Jia

Jia

A Novel of North Korea

BY HYEJIN KIM

midnight
editions

Published in the United States by Midnight Editions, an imprint of Cleis Press Inc., P.O. Box 14697, San Francisco, California 94114.

Printed in the United States.
Cover design: Scott Idleman
Cover photograph: Hiroji Kubota, Magnum.
Text design: Frank Wiedemann
First Edition.
10 9 8 7 6 5 4 3 2 1

Library of Congress Cataloging-in-Publication Data

Kim, Hyejin.
  Jia : a novel of North Korea / by Hyejin Kim. -- 1st ed.
    p. cm.
  ISBN 978-1-57344-275-6 (pbk. : alk. paper)
 1. Political persecution--Fiction. 2. Korea (North)--Fiction. I. Title.
PS3611.I4545J53 2007
  813'.6--dc22   2007012358

Introduction

Almost ten years ago, during a summer spent traveling through England, I met a paunchy middle-aged man on a double-decker bus. When he caught sight of me, bent over from the weight of my backpack, he smiled and asked, "Where are you from?"

"Korea," I replied, clutching the pole next to the door. The next stop was mine.

"Which Korea?"

I frowned; I didn't understand what he meant.

"South Korea or North Korea?"

I was completely thrown. I watched his face for another moment. *South or North?* I wondered.

Showing my bewilderment, I answered, "South" and got off the bus. I stood there for a while, looking back at the bus.

To me, there was just one Korea. My upbringing was strictly anti–North Korea, and discussion of North Korea was shunned. I had never thought of North Korea as a real country and North Koreans as real human beings. In comics and cartoons, North Koreans had red faces or bony features and their leaders were all monsters. Every year, on the anniversary of the beginning of the Korean War, I had to hand in an essay and a painting reviling North Korea. That was the only time I could use my favorite color—red—as much as I wanted.

When I was an infant, my father, a young, passionate history teacher who was curious about other political systems, was convicted of being a North Korean sympathizer. His possession of socialist books was taken as evidence that he worked for the North by the dictators who then ruled South Korea, and his comments to friends and colleagues about problems with the Park Chung Hee administration confirmed to prosecutors that he was a dangerous man. When my father left for prison, my first birthday hadn't yet passed. Seeing my father five years later, when he was finally released, I cried and shouted at him to get out of my house. I remember his bald head terrifying me.

North Korea and the South Korean dictatorship had created a five-year gap in the relationship between father and daughter; my hostility toward him cost my father many tears.

I came to know my father's history when I was 14 years old, when my mom told me his story, and since then I have seen North Korea as both a constant threat and a beguiling Pandora's box, an object of curiosity that we shouldn't open.

Until we can. For me that time came several years ago, when I spent a year living in Shenyang, the hub of northeast China.

On a stifling summer weekend early in my stay, a friend invited me to her grandparents' house. Far from Shenyang, their town lacked modern facilities and seemed to be inhabited chiefly by the elderly.

My friend's grandparents are *chosunjok,* a term that refers to ethnic Koreans who live in China. The province of Liaoning, which borders North Korea, has several *chosunjok* towns, most of which developed with the migration of Koreans to China earlier in the twentieth century, when Japan made the Korean Peninsula a colony. Living together in northeast China, these Koreans have managed to maintain traditional Korean customs in a foreign land. In the past few years, however, the villages have emptied out, as young people like my friend are lured to the city for work.

In the late afternoon, my visit complete, I headed for the bus station, declining my friend's offer to see me off. I didn't want to take a minute of joy away from the wrinkled faces of the two who were hosting their granddaughter. After a two-hour wait at a dusty, windy bus stop, I fought my way on board my ride home; competition to survive among 1.3 billion Chinese begins and ends with getting a seat on the bus. I had already learned to give up hope of ever sitting—there was no way to beat the Chinese people. I decided to stand.

"Sit here." A clear female voice emerged from the surrounding clatter, giving me a small start: someone spoke Korean.

A lovely face smiled, looking up at me. With her hand, she patted a small empty space on her seat. Her strong accent made me think she must be a *chosunjok,* and she probably thought I was one as well. Her big eyes and small hand were poised for my reply. She tried to make a space for me, and when I tried to refuse, she kept smiling, and said, "Why not? It's only going to get more crowded."

That was how I met the woman I have come to call "Jia." As more and more people scrambled onto the bus, just as she had predicted, we exchanged a few polite questions over the screaming and shoving of our fellow passengers. The commotion in the bus was like a small war.

I asked her if she was born in Liaoning.

She replied lightly, "No, I am North Korean."

The instant I heard it, I could feel my heart quicken. *I am talking to a North Korean right now*, I thought; *North Korean, not South Korean.*

"I came here two years ago," she continued.

I smiled at her but couldn't look directly into her eyes. I was afraid somebody had heard what she had said. There might be some North Korean agents among us, who would catch her and take her to the police. My new friend seemed not to care. She asked me where I was heading. We discovered we were both heading to North Station and spent the rest of the ride in silence. Every now and then I stole a glance at her; she had a big bag, but there did not seem to be anything in it.

As the bus began to empty and seats were freed around us, Jia and I stayed put in our shared seat, looking out the window in silence. The tall buildings of downtown Shenyang blocked the strong winds of the outlying area, and the hazy world turned into a clear and colorful one. Eventually we pried ourselves from the seat and stepped off the bus, but our good-bye was not a final one; Jia and I became friends.

What attracted me to her? The purpose of my stay in China was to learn about the Chinese people, not other Koreans—let alone *North* Koreans. Was I motivated by the curiosity that had been building in me for decades? Soon, I learned about Jia and her compatriots, I entered the world of "other Koreans," whose lives had previously been closed off to me. I wanted to tell their stories for many reasons, perhaps the most important one being the simplest: because these other Koreans walk the Earth with us.

The characters in this novel, Jia included, are an amalgam of what I saw for myself in China, what I heard from North Korean border crossers and those assisting them, and what I encountered in my research documenting asylum seekers and North Korean society. My original plan to stay in China for two months was stretched to a year, and during that time, I stumbled across a variety of people with links to North Korea: Chinese-born Koreans who had North Korean neighbors, church groups sympathetic to North Koreans, and activists who took risks to help North Korean border crossers. The last group welcomed me, a curious outsider, on their dangerous trips. At first I felt that observing such underground activities was a lucky opportunity, but as time went on I came to feel that it was my destiny, both as a writer and as a Korean.

Over several months in 2001 and 2002, I met with the woman who was the inspiration for Jia. When we first met, she was quiet and shy, but she had the confidence and tranquility of someone who let her life progress with the flow of time. The more time I spent with her, the more that confidence came to the fore, along with her passion and firm hopes for a better life. Her eyes, full of enthusiasm for the future as well as yearning for lost loved ones, continued to stir my mind long after I left China. They led me to put this story to paper.

My hope is that readers will gain a better understanding of the lives of North Koreans—beyond the lens of geopolitics or ideology—and see what I have seen in one woman's eyes.

Hyejin Kim
Singapore, March 2007

TIME LINE

1905	Jia's grandfather is born
1910, Aug. 29	Japan annexes Korea as a colony
1931	Manchurian Incident: Japan sets up a puppet government in northeastern China
1937	Outbreak of the Sino-Japanese War
1940	Jia's father is born
1943	Jia's mother is born
1945, Aug. 15	Korean liberation from Japan with the end of World War II
1948, Aug. 15	Establishment of the Republic of Korea (South Korea)
1948, Sept. 9	Establishment of the Democratic People's Republic of Korea (North Korea)
1949, Oct. 1	Establishment of the People's Republic of China, led by Mao Zedong
1950, Jun. 25	Korean War begins
1953, Jul. 27	Korean War Armistice Agreement, after American and South Korean forces fight Chinese and North Korean forces to a stalemate
1966	Jia's sister is born
1971	Jia is born
1976, Sept. 9	Death of Mao Zedong
1989	World Festival of Youth and Students in Pyongyang
1994, Jul. 8	Death of Kim Il Sung

1995–1999	Floods in 1995 and 1996 contribute to a famine that kills between 200,000 and 3.5 million and displaces tens or hundreds of thousands to China, Mongolia, Russia, Vietnam, and Thailand
1997, Oct. 8	Kim Jong Il officially assumes the titles General Secretary of the Workers' Party of Korea and Chairman of the National Defense Commission
2004	460 North Koreans arrive in South Korea, after having traveled the length of China to Vietnam, where they were discovered
2006, Aug. 22	In a Bangkok suburb Thai police discover 175 North Koreans hoping for asylum

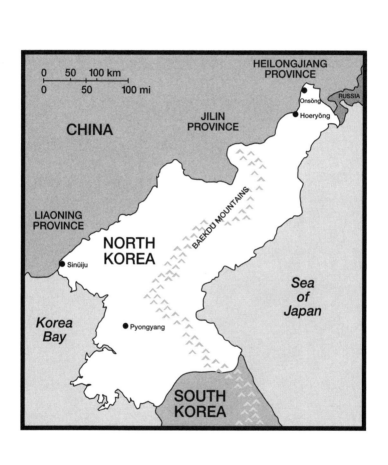

Part 1

1

My Secret Childhood

I don't know when I was born. I don't know whether my mom ever saw my face or just left for the other world without a glimpse of me. I still wonder whether my father is alive or dead. After giving birth to me, my mother didn't get enough to eat—no bowls of *miyeokguk*, no honey, eggs, or pork—not even the most basic food for a woman just out of childbirth. Instead, my grandmother soaked the placenta and umbilical cord in water, drained them of blood (they shrink and turn white), cut them into tiny cubes, and coated them with sugar so that my mom could swallow each piece in one bite. She wasn't supposed to chew, in order to protect her teeth, which were still soft from the punishment of pregnancy, but she was too weak to swallow. In the end, this sustenance didn't help enough; perhaps she didn't want to share this world with me.

My grandmother liked to say I was a troublemaker even in the womb. It seemed I wanted out as soon as possible. My mom often rolled on the floor, clutching her stomach after a flurry of my kicks; they were sure I would be a boy, that I had been a soccer player in my previous life.

My grandmother's face would bloom with a smile when she said, "Jia, you don't know how happy we were when we saw you for the first time. We were so relieved that you were an adorable girl, and not the tough little nut of a boy we were expecting. Your sister and I couldn't handle that, and now I don't have to worry about you going crazy about soccer and coming home injured, like your father did when he was a boy."

My father's and mother's photographs were hidden in a recess of my grandmother's closet. My grandfather didn't allow me to see them, and when he discovered me holding my parents' pictures in my hands, he scolded me bitterly. He also shouted at my grandmother; he didn't know she had held on to them, and that whenever I wasn't feeling well she dandled me on her knee and showed me the photos for comfort. She would talk for hours about my father and mother, their love for each other, and my mother's extraordinary beauty.

In his individual photos, my father never smiled. His thick hair was brushed straight back from his forehead; his eyes were two long slits, staring directly into the camera, as if in challenge. He looked stubborn, with his triangular face and thin lips. In the photos with my mother, however, he was transformed: his eyes turned to half-moons as he smiled; he looked like a bashful boy.

When my father saw my mother for the first time, dancing in her traditional *hanbok* with the grace of a pink-winged butterfly, he fell in love instantly. When I saw the pictures, I envied her big eyes, straight legs, and thin waist. She put on such bright makeup and wore beautiful dresses, and always smiled in her pictures. I wondered if she still smiled in the other world.

My sister also remembered our mother. When my body was feverish, she would hold my hand in bed and talk about her.

"At first, I despised you. I believed you took Mom to the other world. I didn't want to see you or take care of you at all. You would cry for days at a time—you were always hungry, because we couldn't feed you well. I even prayed you would go back to your world and Mom would return in your place. But Jia, you're my treasure now. I can't stand it when you're sick—don't be sick anymore." We fell asleep hugging each other tightly. Her hand was like magic, and my fevers never lasted very long.

When I was small, I came down with any and every disease a child could have. Vomiting was a regular part of my life; fever frequently occupied my body. My grandparents and my sister worried whenever symptoms of a new disease came on, because they couldn't get suitable medicine. Sometimes they had to watch over my ailing body helplessly for several days, never sleeping. I don't get sick easily anymore. Perhaps my trials as a child gave me the strength I have now.

There weren't many people in the part of North Korea where my family lived. Mountains stretched in all directions, and what few people there were fit into either of two categories: "extremely bad" and "commonly bad." The extremely bad were locked inside barbed-wire fences, and the commonly bad lived outside the fence. We were fortunate to be in the second group. The "inside people," as we called them, had faces stained with coal ash and were perpetually bent over, their eyes staring at the ground, no matter how old they were. The men in dark-green uniforms, however, had clean faces and shiny shoes.

My grandparents strictly forbade my sister and me from walking along the fence. Sometimes I looked down at the camp from high up on the hill; I could see the contrasting faces of the residents and the guards.

We didn't talk with our neighbors much. People seemed to be too tired to talk to each other. Adults left their house early and came back with black dust on their faces. My grandfather and grandmother were not exceptions. My grandfather had back trouble and often coughed up phlegm. My grandmother's problems were not as serious, as her job cooking for the white-faced guards in the camp was less dangerous than his. I spent many evenings waiting for her to come home with leftovers, like rice cakes or glutinous rice jelly. "Today was a lucky day for you girls," she would say, shuffling through the door with a wrinkled smile.

Surrounding our house were mountains and an enormous valley, with trees and grass everywhere in between. The water was clean; we could drink it without a care, and my sister and I swam every day. Whenever I wasn't sick, I was outside until late into the evening; I wanted to make up for my bedridden life with outdoor activities. Our grandparents assigned homework daily, usually the collection of mushrooms and herbs. Every night, huddled close together, we cleaned our harvest thoroughly, and the next day our grandparents brought it to the camp. My sister and I spent the days searching the mountains and valleys for new things to do and see. We held races to see who could swim faster; though I was much younger than my sister, my long arms and legs helped me win, or at least get abreast of her. It could be she simply gave me the chance.

I was curious about people and other places, and I read all the books my grandmother kept in her closet. They helped my sister and me forget about the gray faces and the thick, pointy wire fences, even for an hour. The photos in some of the books thrilled me, transporting us to places we had never been and introducing us to people we had never met. I had so many questions about what I saw in the pictures: the high buildings, the people walking on pavement, and especially the kids my own age dressed in nice clothing. These were photos taken in Pyongyang, North Korea's biggest city, and from first sight, I dreamed of living there and walking those streets. My grandmother answered all my questions kindly, explaining everything in detail.

There was only one rule: I was never to ask about my father. My family's refusal to talk about him convinced me he had done something terrible. Often I hugged my grandmother and grumbled that I despised my father, knowing he brought my family tragedy. I knew it was his fault that my mother was dead, and that we lived in such an isolated place. I cursed him over and over, but my grandmother consoled me, whispering that he never meant to hurt us. He was smart, she'd say, he just wasn't lucky. That's why people tried to hurt him. It was not his fault. His only fault was being born in the wrong place.

I learned my parents' story the day before my unexpected farewell to my grandparents and my sister. I didn't even get the chance to boast to my sister about what I had learned from Grandmother. I didn't know it was the last gift she would give to me.

2

My Father's and Mother's Story

Everyone said that my father and mother never should have met, that it was the beginning of a tragic story. My mom was from a good family; as an only child, she was given everything she could have wanted. Her family belonged to the "core class," the highest of the three government-assigned categories. Mom's father occupied a high position in the army, and her mother was a vice principal at a small college. She inherited her father's outstanding physique, and took advantage of it by studying at a professional dancing school.

Dancers shouldn't be afraid to face any kind of dance: that was her dancing philosophy. Wearing the traditional *hanbok*, she was fragile and sweet in her movements, like a flying butterfly, but when she donned a military uniform, her movements expressed the spirit of a strong and passionate revolutionary soldier. Success as a famous dancer was every woman's dream in North Korea. My mother's talent and good background, and the support of her family, suggested that she would become the most famous dancer in Pyongyang. Then she met my father.

It was a bad match. My father, by contrast, had a complicated family: they belonged to one of the lower classes of society, the "wavering class." My great-grandparents on my father's side were exploited by the Japanese in the early part of the century; their mistake was to own too much land and to have too many servants. My grandfather grew up seeing his father regularly beaten by Japanese police and eventually stripped of his property.

When my grandfather was 15, a single incident changed his life forever. A secret guerilla group agitating for independence passed through the town. They were caught by the Japanese police but resisted their captors, eventually killing them. After taking food and weapons from the police warehouse, the group hastily disappeared. The episode left the town's young people excited and anxious.

Several days later, my grandfather disappeared from his house with only these written words: "I'm leaving to be a hero for my country." He went to northeast China and instantly joined a guerrilla group. At that time, it was difficult to stage independence activities against Japan in Korea. Some Koreans protested with their feet, moving to northeast China and joining Chinese nationalist or communist groups. Others conducted their own, purely Korean, activities. There were many young people like my grandfather: passionate about punishing the Japanese.

He didn't take on the colors of any faction, and he wasn't interested in ideology; his purpose was to see how many

Japanese soldiers and policemen he could kill. He and his comrades lurked about in villages at night, looking for targets, and gathered in the mountains during the day. They learned how to make bombs and produce dynamite, using them to punish the Japanese police and the Korean stool pigeons. Their radical strategies made it difficult to get regular financial support from the usual associations that secretly funded such activities. They were always hungry, always cold, as they traveled back and forth between northeast China and the northern tip of Korea.

My grandmother was an obedient student and daughter, but she secretly supported independence activists, providing food for them and helping to write and distribute pamphlets. When my grandfather's guerilla group stayed in the vicinity of my grandmother's town, the underground student association my grandmother belonged to helped them maintain their cover. She was the chief editor of the association at that time. My grandfather and grandmother had never even spoken privately before their marriage. They met only as comrades, with others around.

During these times, a horrible rumor spread through the village. People said the Japanese soldiers were dragging young, single women to the battlefield and using them as whores to console solders tired from battle.

The rumor that the women in my grandmother's village would be targeted threw the village into chaos. Some families with adult daughters believed the Japanese soldiers would never do such a thing; others hurried to find single men willing to marry their girls. My grandfather went directly to my grandmother's house and told her parents that he was taking her with his group when they left town. My grandmother's parents objected strongly; they knew my grandfather's life was dangerous—his life itself was in constant danger. My grandmother overheard the conversation, packed her belongings, and left her house with my grandfather without turning back. They were married before his comrades in the mountains and honeymooned in a cave.

From then on, hard times were their lot. World War II only made conditions worse. Just as the rumors predicted, women were dragged away by the Japanese Army. The Japanese killed anyone they even suspected of being against them. My grandfather's group had to move every day, hiding in the mountains. Moving so often caused my grandmother to lose an unborn child five months into pregnancy and undergo another two consecutive natural abortions. When they finally delivered my father, their only child, in 1943, my grandmother wept for days. Though she was happy to have given birth, she couldn't help but be afraid for my father. When the Japanese were defeated in 1945, she expressed her relief for him by saying, "He can get a regular education, in a normal school."

My grandparents and my father were living in Anshan, then a small city in northeast China, when the Japanese began trickling out of northeast China and Korea. At first, my grandmother resisted the long journey to China because my father was sick, but my grandfather was unhappy about changes in the Korean Peninsula: the Korean fight against Japan had turned into an ideological fight between Korean people, communists in the north and nationalists in the south. Foreign influence in the Korean Peninsula shifted from Japan to the Soviet Union and United States. There were conflicts, arguments, and betrayals among ideologues everywhere in China and Korea. Choosing a side affected people's lives so profoundly that some were found dead the day after switching from one side to the other. Nobody knew who was right, who was wrong.

Five years later, when the Korean War began in 1950, my grandparents were still in northeast China. They feared for their relatives and decided to bring them across the border. When my grandfather returned to Korea to find them, however, he was arrested by the South Korean Army. Despite his insistence that he had no ideological position, his history and his hot temper persuaded his South Korean captors to suspect he was with the North. He was sent to Geoje Island, off the southern coast of South Korea, and held there for several years. My grandmother took my father back to North Korea and found her parents. She looked for her husband but was told he had never arrived. Several years later, when the war ended, the two Koreas exchanged captives, and my grandfather and grandmother reunited in North Korea.

When prisoners of war came back to North Korea, most were welcomed ardently as heroes to the country. But my grandfather's history and lack of ideology were not appreciated by the North Koreans. What is worse, the North Korean government became suspicious of people who had been held in South Korean prisons. Though most of the prisoners were communists, their time in the South made their commitment appear dubious, and they were gradually excluded from important positions.

In spite of my grandfather's revolutionary activities for Korean independence, his life after the war was miserable. He received no compensation for his years in prison, and instead was placed under constant government supervision. Inside the house, he was a hero, but outside he was powerless and considered a possible reactionary element. My father grew up seeing it all, and he became cynical. He was a big man, and energetic, like his father; always the best soccer player, and at the top of his math class. He loved science and reading, but his family background limited and embittered him. While my mother was satisfied with her station in life, having realized her dreams of becoming a dancer, my father recognized that he would never get what he wanted.

My father's talent for science brought him to despair. Although he scored the highest in his school on the university entrance examination, he could not get into the university of his choice. Every year, a set number of students from each province can enter university, and each university decides how many students it will accept from each province, distributing admission tickets to the schools in the province. In my father's year, his school was awarded five tickets from the university where he wanted to study. The examination scores didn't matter much: acceptance hinged on family background. Despite receiving a lower score, my father's competitor in soccer and mathematics since elementary school easily got in, while my father was rejected. He was not a chosen person in his world.

My father's teacher intervened on his behalf, and after negotiations with the Education Bureau, a small college admitted my father on the condition that he would start teaching there as soon as he graduated. My mother's mother, who didn't like my father much, worked in that college. On the school stage, she held him up as an example of the generosity of the country toward reactionary elements, but he failed to demonstrate his appreciation to the audience, which had expected a touching speech from him.

His mind was made for science. He studied and he conducted his research, becoming the youngest teacher in the college. It was then that he met my mother. They ran into each other in the corridor on the way to his laboratory. She had just found out when her next dancing performance at the Grand Theater would be and was stopping by the school to tell her mother.

On seeing my father, my mother approached him and asked, "What do you do here?"

"I've heard I'm regarded as a teacher," he replied curtly.

That night, my mom asked my grandmother to bring all the faculty members to her performance; her intention, of course, was to invite my father. After the performance, they began dating. I don't know how they came to love each other or what they talked about, but Grandmother said my father changed: he smiled more.

When my mother's parents discovered the relationship, they almost killed my father. Such an unbalanced love affair was a slap in their faces. My father lost his job right away and was to be sent to an isolated village to teach in a small school. If my mother had given up my father, I wouldn't be in this world, but she quit everything, including eating.

Her desperate resistance against her parents rescued my father, but in effect she sacrificed herself: my grandparents abandoned their daughter permanently and kept a close watch on my father. The marriage was not welcomed by anyone; even my parents' friends were afraid of being punished for associating with them. The only ones who were happy were my father and mother.

My father's self-respect was as strong as his desire to study; nobody could daunt him. He got his position back in the college, owing to my mother's efforts, but it didn't change his attitude toward the college and toward his in-laws.

A terrible event involving his closest friend, Sungwoo, who had a similar background, only strengthened his resistance to the government. Sungwoo couldn't go to university, so he worked in a factory after graduation. Then, one day, he just disappeared. He had been playing poker with his coworkers during their breaks for some time, though it was prohibited (as a "vestige of Japanese imperialism"); people played anyway, and the local government wasn't strict about it. Sungwoo was an exception. When their game was discovered, his coworkers were let off, but Sungwoo was sent to a political concentration camp. His behavior was said to be against the government; his family didn't have the preferred background, so his sentence was compounded.

My father tried to find Sungwoo, appealing to the central government about the local government's unfair treatment, but to no avail. Sungwoo was simply erased from his community. After that, my father became increasingly cynical. He publicly criticized the research conditions and lack of funding at the college, and he complained that school staff members were busy using the money to curry favor with their superiors. He dismissed the political science classes, which taught the ideology of Kim Il Sung. "What department am I in, science or politics?" he would say. Eventually, he was dragged away by two soldiers and taken to the Investigation Bureau. His worst offense was the possession of foreign science books from prohibited countries. Nobody knew how he got the books; he had sought them out on his own.

The scandal brought trouble to my family. My father cursed the investigators dispatched from the government. He disappeared several days later; the charge was political treason. People said he would be sent to one of the strictest political concentration camps, a place in the mountains, where no one could find him. My mom looked for him, running from village to village, begging her parents for help. At the time, she was pregnant with me: a little sister for her eight-year-old daughter.

Her parents, however, cared more about their status than for their only daughter. Both sets of parents asked her to get a divorce so she wouldn't be soiled with my father's crimes. But my mom also was obstinate, and she refused to leave my father's family. Several days later, a military truck took my mom, my sister, and my father's parents and dropped them in a political offenders' village. They were not allowed to bring any belongings. Their crime was their relation to my father.

The village was located right next to a political concentration camp. My grandparents and my mother worked for the camp, serving the guards. They hoped to run into my father, though they had no confirmation of his whereabouts. The first words they exchanged after returning from work each day were "Have you seen him?" They were not allowed to talk to prisoners; they could only check their faces as they passed.

That is the story of why I never saw my father and spent my childhood in an isolated compound. My mother believed her parents had prevented our family from actually being sent to the camp, and she hoped that someday they would help us return to our regular lives. The girl who could have anything she wanted had now lost everything.

I don't blame my father. I understand why he remained so steadfast. How desperate he must have been when he realized he couldn't live out his passion for study and research!

What had he learned from his own father's history? My grandmother said my father respected my grandfather with his whole heart. They had different interests, but they both believed in being true to their passions.

Life hasn't changed so much since their time. Just as they did, I must do battle with capricious political winds in order to survive each day.

3

A Stranger's Visit

Where we lived, the temperature rose and fell with the wind. Fall was slipping into winter; leaves were falling from the trees, which themselves were becoming shorter and skinnier as the ground grew softer and taller. Piles of leaves meant that it was time to prepare for winter. The cold pinched at our flesh; sometimes the snow was as deep as I was tall. No matter how cold it got, however, I still pressed for my sister to take me outside. My grandparents were worried I might get another disease from exposure, but being stuck inside only made me sicker.

One typical day, I was nagging my sister to take me outside to play while she ate lunch. I often dictated the day's plan to her, usually including swimming in the pond for two hours or finding five grasshoppers per person. She kept silent, and I watched her spoon move up and down.

That meant "no." I was persistent. I was such a willful girl, and my sister never rejected my begging. She was usually nice to me, but on that day I pinched her arm ceaselessly. Whenever she tried to take a bite, I tapped her right elbow and ran away. In a fit of anger, she finally threw her spoon in my direction, and it smacked me right on the forehead. I was frightened and cried out for Grandmother. My grandmother was startled by my scream, and by the time she entered the room, a big bump had already swelled up on my forehead. My sister seized with fear, grabbed my hand, and both of us flew outside. I was happy, no matter the bump on my head; I had won.

While we walked, she pouted. "I don't feel like going outside today. I had a bad dream: you ran away like Mom did. You didn't turn around even though I shouted to stop you."

Maybe she thought the dream meant something would happen to us. Maybe she intuitively felt that that day might change our lives.

As always, we went to the hills, where we liked to play, but my sister was much stricter than usual; she wouldn't let me out of her sight. Squatting, she watched me idly as I played, rolling on the ground and stomping on leaves. Eventually I dragged her to the valley. The water was cold, but I didn't care. I tried to take off my clothes to swim. She pulled my arms and warned me, her eyes glaring, "No. Swimming season is over. From today, we're not going to swim until next summer."

We sat in silence. "Didn't you hear something from over there?" she asked, repeatedly.

I grew bored because she wouldn't play at all; she insisted on keeping a sharp lookout. Nothing happened—her worrying seemed useless—and on the way home I muttered to her, "You are weird today. You screwed up everything. It's the most boring day I've ever had."

Still she looked around and spoke under her breath. "No, Jia. I'm serious. I swear with my ten fingers. I heard something around us several times."

The days were growing shorter. By the time we arrived at the house, it was already dark, but it wasn't any different from an ordinary night. My sister didn't seem relieved until we finished dinner and played our favorite word game, where you link the last syllable of one word to a new word. Grandmother was always on my side; otherwise, there was no way to beat my sister. She grumbled about Grandmother's help and tried to get Grandfather on her team.

Just as we were tiring of the game, a low sound came through the door. Only my sister heard it. She swiftly glanced toward the door and gave Grandfather a scared look. "Did you hear, Grandpa?"

He turned to my sister. "What? Did you hear something?"

A moment later, the sound reached our ears clearly. We looked toward the door all at once. Nobody stopped by our house at that time of night. In fact, we never had any visitors at all.

"Who is it?" Grandmother asked Grandfather in a low voice, a startled look in her eyes. I tried to stand up, but my sister pressed me down.

The sound came again. Grandfather turned toward the door. "Who is it?"

"Can I come in? Please..." A man's voice, beyond the door.

We watched each other's faces. I said to Grandfather, "Open the door. It's cold out."

He hesitated for a moment and then opened the door cautiously.

There was a man standing in the doorway. He wore an army uniform.

"Do you have something to eat?"

His skinny face was darkly stained, as though he washed with soot. He clasped his hands in front of his stomach, as if to show he meant no harm. If we were frightened of a stranger's unexpected visit, he seemed even more frightened by the encounter.

"We don't have any food that would satisfy you."

"It's okay. I can eat anything. I haven't eaten for two days."

With that, Grandfather let him in. He looked around the room restlessly before sitting down right in front of the door. My sister stepped behind her and stuck to the wall, dragging me next to her. She held my hand tightly.

Grandfather said to Grandmother, "Bring some food he can eat." She looked at him with suspicious eyes and slid into the kitchen without a word.

"Thank you," the man said. I remember thinking he had a funny way of speaking. I tried to get a closer look at him, but my sister warned me, giving me sharp pinches.

"I've become lost." He took off his hat and pointed a finger at us. "I followed those kids all day. Otherwise, I would have wandered around the mountains for one more night."

My sister opened her eyes wide and looked at me to let me know that she had been right about hearing noises during the day.

The man gave us a smile, and I smiled back at him. He didn't look like a bad guy.

Grandfather told us to offer our seats. That was the warmest place in the room, where my sister and I always sit. We moved next to Grandfather, and I finally got out of my sister's grip. Grandmother opened the kitchen door and asked Grandfather, "Do you want me to heat up the fireplace?"

The stranger shook both his hands to stop my grandmother. "No. It's warm enough. You don't have to...I mean it. This is already heaven to me. Sorry to give you such trouble."

A little later, Grandmother set the table. I stood up nimbly and took the dishes from her hands, asking the soldier with a smile, "Do you want some plain water or scorched rice water? I recommend my grandmother's scorched rice water—it's really good." I didn't care about my sister anymore, and I dodged her gaze.

"Thank you. Either one is fine," he said, smiling, showing his white and well-arranged teeth.

I brought him some fairly hot scorched rice water. Grandmother always made it, boiling the leftover cooked rice, stuck in the pot, in water for a long time over a low fire. We sipped it before or after our actual meal because it made our stomachs warm and full. It was too hot to drink in one stretch, and sometimes I burned my tongue. I couldn't understand how my grandparents could drink something so hot and then say, in a satisfied voice, "Hu! How cool it is!"

When I asked them how they could refer to such a hot drink as cool, they tried to explain. "Even though it's hot, when it goes down along your throat and arrives at your stomach, you can feel it make your insides so clean and cool." Seeing my dissatisfaction, they would grin and say, "You'll understand when you grow up."

The soldier sat at the table and wolfed down his food as we all looked on quietly. He said, "I'm taking a guerilla training course that is supposed to last for three months. It's my first time in these mountains—we just arrived here five days ago. When I was doing an individual exercise, I got lost."

While the man spoke, Grandfather rolled a cigarette with thin paper he brought from the mines. "There is an army training camp," Grandfather replied. "I know where it is. Crossing the mine is a shortcut to get there. I'll take you over there." He put the cigarette on the table for the stranger and made another for himself.

"Thanks. It was lucky to run into those kids. I was thinking of asking for help as soon as I saw them, but I was afraid they might be scared. So I followed them and was hesitating at the door."

Grandfather looked at him closely. "Are you a professional soldier? You look a little old to be going through guerilla training for the first time."

Putting the spoon and chopsticks down on the table, he nodded slightly to my grandmother as a token of gratitude. He watched all of us and cautiously answered, "No. I'm not. I was a fisherman. Actually, I'm from South Korea."

I could feel my grandfather's and grandmother's faces suddenly go stiff. And my sister grabbed my hand with such force that I yelped with pain. I didn't know why his answer provoked such a reaction; I knew my country was called North Korea. But it seemed that I was the only one who couldn't really figure out the meaning of what he said, and nobody explained it to me. Feeling an ache in my fingers, I cried out to my sister, "Ouch! You're killing my fingers! Why are you doing that?"

My grandfather became animated and nervous, and he turned to Grandmother and said, "Why haven't you cleared the table? He is already finished."

She stood up hastily, grabbing the dishes. "Right, what am I doing? Dying is what the old do best," she said—a typical elderly Korean response.

My sister started to help, but with a serious face Grandfather ordered us to bed. "It's already late. Sleep!" My sister unfolded a blanket in the corner of the room, hanging her head, but still stealing glances at the soldier.

Grandfather said to the stranger, "Let me know when you want to leave."

The man replied, with consternation, "I will not hurt your family. Anyhow, I'm in North Korea now. And I'm not trying to decamp. I'll go back to the unit—it'll be okay."

The soldier and my grandparents stayed up all night, talking. I tried not to sleep, forcing my eyes open wide. I wanted to hear what they were saying. I sat next to the stranger, propped up against his knee, but my eyelids grew heavy, and at length I fell asleep there. I heard him say he had come to North Korea a year before, on a deep-sea fishing vessel. The ship was fishing close to Chinese waters; what they ran into was not abundant fish, but an armada that glittered with a strange light. More than ten Chinese soldiers boarded his ship. According to them, his ship had violated international law. All the sailors, including him, were taken to North Korea that night. There, he and his comrades were forced to attend ideology classes and military training in the mountains where we lived. During the maneuvers, he became lost.

When I opened my eyes again, it was already morning. The soldier was gone. I was lying next to my grandmother, who was about to leave for the camp. I got up in a flurry and demanded, "Where is he? Where did he go?"

"He already left. Your grandfather sent him off. But he said he'll come back."

I waited for the soldier for several days, but he didn't return. He was the first visitor to our house, and his arrival had stirred a strange excitement in me; his accent was so new and curious.

Several days later, at night, he returned. As with his first visit, we heard a cautious knock at the door. I jumped for joy at seeing him again, and leaped into his arms. He smiled broadly.

He visited our house several times but never could stay long. It was strictly prohibited for him to be absent without leave. He sneaked out of his guard post and came to see us, sometimes bringing army food for my sister and me. I always cried when he left. I wasn't sure whether I would see him again.

Whenever he visited us, my grandparents and he always discussed North Korea and South Korea. It was hard to understand what they were really saying; they spoke in such soft voices and used words I had never heard before. My grandfather never showed his feelings on his face, but it was easy to see how happy the soldier's visits made him. Grandmother said he was about my father's age and had a seven-year-old girl, the same age as me, in the South. Perhaps I reminded him of his daughter. He always propped me on his knee while he was in my house, checking on my studies. I took to calling him Uncle Shin, a nickname that indicated an almost familial closeness.

After several weeks, Uncle Shin said the army was leaving soon. My grandparents just nodded quietly, and we didn't talk about his leaving that night, but the next day I began asking my grandparents if we could go with him. I remembered he said he had been in Pyongyang, the capital, and I whimpered that I wanted to go to the city and live there. They only patted my head.

The day before Shin was to leave, my grandfather called me softly, looking outside through the open door. Grandmother had taken my sister to the mountains to pick some herbs for dinner. I was sulking about being left behind.

Grandfather sat me in front of him and said, "Jia, do you want to go to school?"

I was taken aback by the sudden question, but I instantly said, "Yes."

"Do you want to meet your mom's parents?"

"The people wearing good clothes in the pictures? Yes, sure." Quickly, I covered my mouth with both hands, because I was not supposed to know about the pictures. He ignored my admission and rolled a cigarette, casting his eyes down. "If you go with Uncle Shin, you can study in a nice school, meet Mom's parents, eat very well, and have lots of toys and clothes. If you stay here with us, you can't meet good teachers or have lots of friends. Do you want to go with him?"

"Okay."

He seemed a bit surprised by my easy, instant reply but merely took a deep pull on his cigarette. A little later, my grandmother and sister returned empty-handed, having found no herbs.

That night, my grandmother put my clothes in a small, gray, decrepit bag. Leading me to the kitchen, she gave me my grandparents' and my mother's pictures. One photograph, taken when my sister was just born, showed my mother holding her infant in her arms. This picture was my sister's most valuable possession.

"In the place you're going, show these pictures and say these are your grandparents and your mother. If people ask you where you are from, what your parents are doing, and where they are, don't say anything. Just say you don't remember. Don't talk to strangers before you meet your grandparents. Just tell them you have pictures and you know they are of your grandparents and mom, and that the baby is you. Say you have to meet them. The pictures will definitely take you to your grandparents. Okay? Erase your whole memory of this place. You'll miss us, but don't ask other people to take you back here—it might put our lives at risk. It's for your safety and our safety. You understand, Jia?"

I couldn't understand why they were so serious, but I nodded my head on and on. It was then that Grandmother told me the story of my parents, how they fell in love and why they were torn apart. She assured me that my mother's death was natural, and not my fault. My grandmother was treating me like an adult, and it delighted me.

That night, Uncle Shin came back, and my grandmother served him a whole table full of dishes. My sister and I were beside ourselves at the sight of all the food: *jangjolim* (beef boiled in soy sauce) and steamed potato with glazed millet jelly, which we only ate on special days, like the Great Leader's birthday. As we wolfed the food down noisily, I completely forgot about leaving and the conversations with my grandparents.

Tapping my stomach, filled to satisfaction, I fell asleep as usual while they talked. In the middle of the night, my body was shaken awake, and when I opened my eyes I saw only my grandmother's face close to mine. She spoke in a whisper, "Jia. Get up. You have to leave right now."

I tried to rub the sleep out of my eyes; I didn't expect it so soon.

"Where?"

"Get up. Put these clothes on."

She dressed me hurriedly. I was still so sleepy. "Do I have to go right now?"

"Yes—there's no time."

Still I rubbed my eyes, looking for my sister. She was in a deep slumber next to me, "How about Sister?"

With flushed cheeks, Grandmother buttoned my dark-green coat—my sister's favorite. "She is not going right now. Hurry." She led me by my hand outside.

Uncle Shin and Grandfather were already outside waiting for me. Everything was dark. I asked my grandfather, again, "Is my sister going with me?" I didn't want to leave by myself, though I was happy to go anywhere with Uncle Shin.

"No. She's not going to go." Grandfather strapped my small bag on my back.

Uncle Shin stooped to level his eyes with mine. He smiled and rubbed my head. "Ready to go?"

"Why do we have to go right now? Let's go later. It's still night."

Uncle Shin took my hand, still rubbing my eyes. "No… it's already late. Let's go right now, Jia."

He exchanged brief words with my grandparents; my grandfather patted his shoulder. My grandmother hugged me tightly and my grandfather stood up next to her, smoking. With a blank face, he said, "Don't forget what we told you, Jia."

I couldn't even say good-bye to my sister. When I looked back, my grandparents were just two dark lumps under the starlight. They didn't move until my eyes lost sight of them.

I couldn't walk very well in the dark; Uncle Shin carried me on his back, walking fast, and talked about his daughter. Half asleep, I heard only part of what he said.

"I never carried my daughter on my back. Can you believe that? I was such a strict father. I always wanted to kiss her cheek and hug her, but I just didn't. I didn't know how to express my feelings about her. She was my treasure…such a treasure. I was not a good father, but she always jumped on me whenever I came home, like you did."

I wondered if my father would carry me on his back, if he saw me just one time.

We had been walking for quite some time when Uncle Shin suddenly stopped and looked around. Emerging from the bushes, we came to a big road, and he took me down from his back, holding my two arms before me.

"Jia, just sit down here and don't move. Wait for two army cars to come. When you see them, sit up and wave your hands. If you see me among those soldiers, pretend you don't know me, just say you're lost. Whatever they ask, say you don't remember anything and ask us to take you to your home, then show the pictures and say they're your grandparents. Do you understand, Jia? I know you are a very smart girl. I know it will be scary to be here by yourself, but it's just for a few hours. After that, we'll take you to your grandparents safely."

He gave me rice balls with sesame oil and salt and a brown red-bean cake.

"If you feel hungry, eat these."

Uncle Shin sat me by the road at the edge of the bushes. It was almost dawn.

As he ran away, uphill, he turned back and shouted, "It'll be bright soon! Don't be scared!"

Then he disappeared from sight.

I was totally alone. It was cold and there was nothing but trees and grass in every direction. I had never been so far away from home, and the path I was on lay far beyond the realm that I knew, back in the forest. I looked back at the world that had been my home; now, from the outside, it no longer felt familiar. Tall reeds swayed in the wind. I heard the occasional stirring of cicadas in the bushes. Starting and then falling silent, the more the insects cried, the closer they seemed to me. I was frightened an animal would appear in front of me and attack me.

I began sobbing, crumpling with fear. I missed my sister and grandparents. I didn't know what I was doing. I couldn't understand why I had to meet my mom's parents this way. After I had exhausted myself I lay down on the road, curled up, and fell asleep.

I didn't hear the cars pull up and stop in front of me. One of the men nudged me with his boots, and I woke up to find soldiers all around, looking down at me.

"Hey, kid. What are you doing here?"

I was confused, I thought I was still in our room at home, lying next to my sister, but my surroundings were strange. I couldn't answer his question. I was too scared to talk at all, and froze until my eyes fixed on Uncle Shin. He was almost covered by the other soldiers, but at the sight of me, he smiled slightly, his eyes filled with worry. As soon as I found his face, I remembered the night journey and falling asleep alone in the darkness. I burst into tears, not out of fear, but comfort—relieved that I had discovered him.

"Look at this girl…"

One soldier sat down to console me. He had bushy eyebrows that wriggled along above his eyes like two pine-eating caterpillars whenever he spoke. He stood me up, dusted off my coat, and said, "Why do you sleep here? Where's your house?"

"I don't know where I am. I'm looking for my grandparents," I sobbed.

"How did you get here?"

"I don't know. Take me to my grandparents."

I wanted to go back to the mountain. I missed my grandparents and wanted to jump into their arms.

"Do you have your birth ID?" he took the backpack from my back and handed it to another soldier next to him, who opened it to search inside.

"No. I don't have it."

Their faces wore worried looks.

"Where do they live?"

I looked at Uncle Shin. His eyes tried to say something through his nervous countenance. I followed my grandmother's instruction exactly: "Pyongyang." His head nodded slightly with a smile.

"Do you live there?" The bushy-eyebrow man gave a suspicious look. I nodded my head lightly.

"But why are you here right now? This is far away from Pyongyang—a kid can't get here alone."

"I don't know. I was here when I opened my eyes. Take me to my grandparents," I wailed.

"How can we find them?"

The soldier searching my backpack handed the pictures to the bushy-eyebrow man, and the other soldiers moved in to look at them.

"How can we find them with these pictures?"

The soldiers made a fuss about that, and the bushy-eyebrow man stood up. Uncle Shin spoke out from behind, "Let's take her with us. We can ask some government offices to find her grandparents."

"No, it's too much hassle. She may be from the limited area close to here," the bushy-eyebrow soldier murmured, touching his chin.

The soldier holding the pictures looked at them one more time. "But look at these—her grandfather is obviously a general with a high position. We'd better take her to the government office—they'll take care of her."

The bushy-eyebrow man hesitated and looked at me for a while, his eyebrows undulating with thought. He gathered the pictures and put them back into my backpack. "Is there anything else in there?"

"No, just some clothes, nothing else," the soldier said, shrugging his shoulders.

"Take her in the car. Let's move. Get in the cars, men. Hurry, we're late now!"

I got in the same car as Uncle Shin, and he told the others he'd take care of me. He held my hand without a word, but when the car started moving, he whispered, "Good girl. You did a good job. You'll meet your grandparents soon," and rubbed my back softly. I wanted to say how scared I was during the night and that I wanted to go back to the mountain, but sitting next to him, all I felt was relief, and I held his hand tightly. I rebuffed the soldiers' questions until they grew tired of asking, and gave me whatever food they had in their pockets. Uncle Shin pulled a khaki cotton blanket over my legs and hugged me tightly.

I fell asleep, but awoke with a start several times. I kept having nightmares of my grandparents and sister being tied together by a thick metal chain and dragged into a deep cave. My sister stared at me and cursed, *Everything is because of you. Because of you...* I cried out, *I'll go with you. Don't leave me!* But my grandfather called down to me, *Don't come here. You're not part of our family anymore.* Then they left together and disappeared, leaving me in the middle of a terrific darkness.

I awoke, choked with tears, crying, "Grandmother! Grandfather! Don't leave me!" The soldiers thought I was crying for the grandparents in the pictures, and Uncle Shin cradled me until I fell asleep.

I awoke the final time to his words, "Jia, get up! We've arrived in Pyongyang."

I opened my eyes and looked toward the open back of the truck.

The car was still moving—not on the rugged mountain path, but on even asphalt. There were high buildings in all directions, and a big golden statue, stretching its arm up to the sky, came in sight. That was my first glimpse of Pyongyang.

Part 2

4

Second Life

"Is your name Jia?"

"Yes."

"How old are you?"

"According to the document, she is sixteen."

The director of the orphanage answered the questions for me. The strangers—three men and two women—looked through the document for several minutes. All the men wore gray jackets in the same style; their appearance gave them away as government officials. The women's clothes contrasted sharply with the men's. I'd never seen so many colors on one person. The older woman wore a light red silk blouse and a black skirt. Her glasses, with their small, thin lenses, looked as sharp as her eyes. She held a small black handbag on her right arm, and all her small accessories seemed to be made for her tiny physique. The other woman wore a simple, light-blue shirt and a gray skirt. Their outfits didn't match their surroundings at all; I was curious how they got such clothes.

The eldest of the men peered at the document through black, thick-rimmed spectacles. The woman with the red blouse stood up briskly from her worn-out brown chair. It was like a small red coil springing from the ground. With her outfit, I guessed her to be around 40 (though I later learned she was over 50); her body was still perfectly balanced, still fit. Walking in my direction, she took a good look at me from top to bottom before grabbing my shoulder slightly and spinning me around clockwise. Extending my arms, she said to herself, "Such long arms and legs. Those will be big advantages."

"She is too old to learn now. She has never had regular training in a professional school," the oldest man said, raising his head from my identification papers.

The woman assessing my body threw her head back, exclaiming, "What do you know about this field? It's not too late—she could catch up. We're not looking for a lead dancer anyway, we just need more dancers. The director already said she's the best one here, and we saw her performance. What else do we need?"

Ignoring the man's pout, she turned back to me. She took several steps back. I was baffled, and felt suddenly naked; my face flushed. She really had sharp eyes: their apple shape and long slant made them even stronger. Not a strand of hair stuck out of her ponytail. Seeing her up close, I thought she looked much older than I had first assumed. She went back to her seat, and, on sitting down, sighed and said, "Sing whatever you want."

I stood up, looking dully at the director of the orphanage

and the others in turn. Why would they want to hear my song? The director had called me to stop by her office after lunch, only to bring me to the room where these people were waiting. I was bewildered; I stalled.

Losing patience, the director stalked over to me and whispered, "Jia. Sing the song you think is the best for your voice." She grabbed my left hand and yanked me forward, in front of them. "She will sing. She's just a little nervous." She signaled me again, with an urging eye.

I sang the Third Aria from the opera *Girl Selling Flowers*. As I sang, I remembered I had seen these same people the previous weekend, at the performance to welcome the government officials on their regular visit. Every year, the orphanage held a performance to entertain visiting officials. As I voiced the lyrics of the song, I tried to figure out why I was there. The woman studied me with her hands clasped, bobbing one of her crossed legs.

"Okay. That's enough. Show us your dancing." Waving at me, the sharp-eyed woman stopped me in midsong. "You prepared the audio, right?" she said, turning to the director.

The director seemed more nervous than I was. Her stout body wasn't meant for rushing; she nearly toppled to the floor in her haste to get to the tape recorder on her desk. "Which music do you want?" the director asked me softly.

Before I could ask what music she had, the sharp-eyed woman interrupted, "No. Don't turn it on." She crossed her arms. "Show us the dancing part of the song you just sang."

Whenever we had performances in the orphanage, I took the girl's part in *Girl Selling Flowers*. I was used to singing and dancing in front of audiences, but in that room, at that moment, with only six people's eyes focused on me, I was more anxious than I had ever been. I glanced at the director, but her eyes were busy darting around, checking the reactions of the others and then looking tensely back at me. Something must have happened between them before I arrived.

"Okay. That's enough. Go sit down over there." The sharp-eyed woman pointed to a chair next to the window.

I immediately stopped dancing, crossed the room to sit down, and heaved a sigh of relief. They talked together intently, the tops of their heads forming a circle. I couldn't make out what they were discussing; their faces were inexpressive. The director joined their conversation and occasionally threw me a glance, bobbing her head repeatedly.

The oldest man turned his head to me and asked abruptly, "Do you remember anything about your family or where you lived before you were seven?"

"No," I said, shaking my head, folding my hands on my knees.

"Stand up when you answer our questions," the sharp-eyed woman ordered, and I sprang to my feet. Surely, she was the scariest person I had ever met. "When did you learn to dance?"

I stood at attention. "Three years after I came here."

"She was really good," the director said. "She had never been schooled in dance or singing. One day when she passed a classroom, she saw a group of students practicing dancing. She just copied the older students' dancing in front of the door, but she was like a tiny flying butterfly." The director lavished praise on me, gazing at me with a warm smile. It was true: if she hadn't seen me in the hall that day, I never would have started dancing professionally.

They didn't respond, or even look at the director.

"So...she might be from the reactionary class," the oldest man muttered to himself, without taking his eyes from my document.

The sharp-eyed woman nervously tapped the handbag on her knees. "What are you talking about? I told you I've already made a decision. I'm the one who trains students; I'll decide whether we'll take her or not."

The man looked unsatisfied. "Whatever you want.... But bear this in mind: you may be wasting your time. I'll report her to the department as a possible risk, and if she isn't approved, you'll have to handle it on your own."

She stood up and said, "I'm not going to use her for the main part. I just need more extras and stand-ins. We don't have time to be so picky." The others stood up as well, and the sharp-eyed woman turned to me and said, "We'll take you tomorrow. Pack your things. You're not going to come back here for a while, or forever. So take everything that belongs to you."

As soon as she finished, she left the room, holding her bag on her forearm. The oldest man accompanied her, shaking his head, his hands folded behind his back. The others snickered into their sleeves and followed. The director hurried behind them. Their departure finally left me with some space to breathe, and I felt all my muscles loosening. I tried to stand up, but sunk down wearily into a chair. They had demanded I do several things with no explanation; truly, they were typical representatives of their government.

"What's going on here?" I muttered to myself.

We had made so many preparations for the annual visit of the government officials. Two months earlier we had begun to put the building in order. For the performance, I danced a fan dance, sang in an opera, and then played the accordion. The performers were divided into three groups: traditional dancers, revolutionary dancers, and musicians. Sixty orphans had been chosen for the performance.

For the finale, all the performers appeared on stage and played the "Song of General Kim Il Sung" (*kimilsung jang-gun ui norae*) on accordions, and then the whole audience sang together as the accordion players walked into the audience, praising the Great Leader's achievements.

The rehearsals had required so much time and effort, but the performance itself was over in a matter of hours, and afterward the government officials shot out of the auditorium like arrows. They had applauded, given us flowers, and handed out a few wan compliments. Then their cars disappeared. The performance season was officially over. Returning to our rooms, we collapsed on our beds. The following day was quiet, and we had no classes or activities for the next few days.

On the day when the government officials came again to see me, I had gone in the morning to the dancing hall, but none of the other orphans were there. I knew that, after the performance, the others were sick of that place and wouldn't go there for a while.

Alone, I practiced the part of *Girl Selling Flowers* that I especially liked. Bending my arm as though holding a flower basket, I stretched the other arm toward the sky. I sang the passage where the lead, Kkot-bun, begs passersby to buy flowers. Kkot-bun's devotion to her family saddened me. At least she had a family near her.

When, with a heavy heart, I returned to my room from the dancing hall, I found a message saying the director wanted me in her office right after lunch. But I didn't expect I would meet those strangers in her office.

As I rose to my feet, still shaking from the impromptu performance, the director returned to the office. She rushed straight to me and grasped my hands. "Oh! I'm so proud of you, Jia. You don't know how happy I am right now." Her reddish round face beamed with pleasure.

I was taken aback. "What's going on here, Director? Who were those people? Why did they come here?"

She held my arms more tightly and brought her face close to mine. I couldn't help but grunt from the pain, but she didn't care. "They are all government officials in the art and propaganda department. Jia, they are really high-positioned people. In your life, you would never have the chance to talk to them. Now, they are totally crazy about preparing for the World Festival of Youth and Students, the big festival next year. People all over the world will come to see our Great Leader and the happy life we live under the Great Leader, and we will welcome them with our dancing performances. Isn't that exciting!"

The director's face glowed a deeper red.

"The government officials are looking for fourteen-to-eighteen-year-old girls in every school. Every year they select girls who have dancing and singing talent, and of course, who have a good figure. They saw your performance last weekend, and this morning I got the call. Everything went so well! I still can't believe it. They'll take care of you, they'll train you as a professional dancer. Jia—it's a once-in-a-lifetime opportunity. This is especially rare in the orphanage. You should be grateful to the government; you're a chosen person now. You'll participate in the official dancing group for the festival—they handle the best dancing group in the country. The Great Leader will see your dancing—I knew it. I knew they would take you. I knew it."

She hugged me several times, until her big glasses nearly slipped off her small nose. My body staggered in the director's arms. My heart trembled. *Am I leaving? Am I really leaving?*

At noon the next day, as I left the orphanage, the director cried and held my hands. I couldn't help but break down in tears too; she was like a mother to me. Unable to have a baby of her own, she was the only one who opened her heart and regarded the orphans as her own children. The teachers treated us like trash. No one cared about us, because no one needed us.

I was already 16; the only reason I had been able to stay longer than other orphans, who usually departed before they were 14, was to teach the younger kids how to dance. Otherwise, I already would have been a garbage collector, or a factory cook.

As the car departed, I watched the gray buildings of the orphanage I thought I might never leave grow smaller. I had been stuck in those dismal buildings for ten years. I still remembered the day I arrived—it was as clear as yesterday in my mind.

Following our arrival in Pyongyang, the soldiers took me directly to the orphanage. When the army cars pulled up in front of the high building, Uncle Shin helped me out of the car, and I saw a middle-aged woman with a round face, round glasses, and a round belly bounce toward us. Several people followed her out while, with flushed cheeks, she talked to the bushy-eyebrow soldier. Eventually she nodded her head and approached me, reaching her moist hand out to mine. "Come here, baby," she said. "We'll take care of you."

Saying farewell to the soldiers, I broke into tears, grabbed Uncle Shin's pants, and plopped down on the ground. He looked embarrassed.

The other soldiers made fun of him. "That kid has already grown fond of you—just take her as your daughter."

Before he got back in the car, he hugged me and whispered softly, "They'll take you to your grandparents' house—this is the biggest orphanage in Pyongyang. Don't worry, Jia. Forget everything you remember about the mountain. You'll have a new life here." He squeezed my hands tightly and looked into my eyes. "Jia, you'll have a good life." He promised he would stop by the orphanage soon, but that was the last time I saw Uncle Shin.

Nightmares haunted me at the orphanage. I saw my grandparents and my sister in our house. My sister massaged my grandfather's back and shoulders with her feet. My grandmother sewed worn-out clothes, frowning and complaining that her eyes were getting worse. They all seemed so peaceful despite my absence. I was in a rage, and I scolded them for abandoning me because I was such a troublemaker. They ignored my crying and turned off the light to go to bed. In the darkness, I sobbed alone.

In another dream, they looked horrible and wore sad faces. My sister wouldn't even look at me. She stood with her back to me, holding Grandmother's hand, and I called her again and again, but she wouldn't turn around. Finally, my grandmother took her up in her arms and they left together. My midnight shrieking made me a problem child; I woke up the other orphans.

The director asked me to give her the pictures I had brought. I was reluctant to hand all of them over, but she said it was possible to find my grandparents with them, though it might take some time. I was certain that within a few days I would leave that place and be rescued by my grandparents.

I slept with 25 other kids—all my age—boys and girls mixed in one big dormitory that was little more than a cold floor. When I entered the room the first time, a boy made fun of me, saying, "Didn't you run away from home? Your stepmom picked on you every day, right? Didn't they feed you? Poor you. How easily you were caught by those scary soldiers! Your parents will come here and beat you soon."

I didn't care about him. I was sure I wouldn't be there for long anyway. Unlike the boys, the girls were nice; they asked me how old I was and invited me to play jump rope and jacks, games I had played with my sister every day. I was good at jump rope, while my sister was much better at jacks. We tied one side of the rope around a skinny tree, and one of us held the other side at the same height. Then we'd skip over the rope from ankle height, then knee height, hip, waist, shoulder, neck, and up to the crown of the holder's head. I loved that game. We sang as we skipped. When we felt bored with the same songs we composed our own. We even made up arm gestures to make the game more complicated. We took our jump-rope games so seriously that we frequently got into big arguments.

One day, when it had been raining since early morning, some of the kids were playing jacks inside, while others took a nap. I was strolling around, sulking, when the director came into the room, and had me stand still. She took the cleanest clothes out of my backpack and dressed me up. Patting my cheek lightly, she said my grandparents were coming soon. Before the other kids, I left the room exultant, in a flutter of excitement. I tried not to forget the names of the places I wanted to go.

I watched through the window of the director's office as a shiny black car made its smooth approach to the building. An old couple slipped out of the car: the old man was tall and wore a dark-green military uniform, holding his round military hat at his side; the lady was tiny, and had a round face. Next to him, she was like a cicada on an oak tree. I couldn't see their faces very well. Once I saw them head to the gate, I returned to my chair and waited for them, sitting properly and organizing my tangled hair. Soon the director opened the door, and they stepped into the office awkwardly, walking slowly toward me.

They were the people in the pictures. Though they looked much older, I recognized their faces easily. How many times had I seen those pictures! As they approached, I gave a big smile. I was certain they were my mom's parents, I could feel her in them. They had much better skin and clothes than my grandparents on the mountain. I wanted to tell my sister what was happening in front of me right at that moment. She had never seen them; it was the first time I experienced something before she did.

They sat down on two chairs placed in front of me and looked at me silently for some time. My new grandfather asked the director to excuse us for a minute. She nodded and quietly left the office. Closing the door, she waved a hand over her flushed face, and I answered her by showing my teeth in delight.

Alone, they examined me again. My new grandfather's

air was so brusque, so different from my other grandfather. He looked too clean. He might not have any special smell, and I wondered whether it would be possible to fall asleep next to him, breathing in his smell and tugging on the drooped flesh around his Adam's apple, as I did with my grandfather on the mountain. I didn't dare to watch his face. Moving my fingers, I counted the different-colored medals on his chest. After counting 20, I became worried for him; it must be heavy to carry all of them on his body every day.

With tearful eyes, Grandmother stretched her hand toward me to touch my head. When Grandfather cleared his throat, she pulled her hand back to her knee. Finally, he broke the silence.

"How did you get here from so far away?"

"Some soldiers helped me."

Why did he look so uncomfortable? It seemed he wasn't happy to see me at all.

"Bookchang is too far away for a kid like you to get here alone," he murmured.

"How's your mom?" Grandmother asked, hesitantly.

"I've never seen her. She died when she gave birth." I was surprised at the question. Could they not know about their daughter's death?

Grandmother gasped and turned her head to her husband's side. His face stiffened. He demanded, "How did you get those pictures? Did your grandparents let you come here? Did they send you?"

With my mouth half open, I looked at each of them in turn. Grandmother avoided my eyes; I knew he was blaming my grandparents on the mountain and me as well. His face was turning red, and I didn't want to hear his reproach;

these two people had never cared for me and now they couldn't even spare me a warm look. My cheeks were starting to burn.

"They gave me those pictures to find you because they didn't know where you were. They were right. Without them, I may not have met you at all." I tried to smile at them.

Grandfather said, "What do they want? To get out of the compound? They want us to save them even though they killed my daughter? Isn't it enough to wreck our family? They still don't understand. Do they think they can have their way with us? No! They are much better off than other dissidents, and it's because of me. We tried to be generous because of our daughter—maybe that's not necessary anymore." He gave me a fierce scowl, his face turning purple. He was different from my grandfather on the mountain, like a stranger, and I pulled back in fright.

My grandmother grabbed his arm. He breathed heavily and stopped scolding me. Still, he kept a hard face. He stood up from the chair and said, "We promised the government we would have no contact with you. We swore that we didn't have a daughter in our lives. You and your grandparents don't realize that your behavior could risk all of our lives."

He lowered his voice and continued, "We don't have a daughter. We don't have any granddaughter either." He turned back and left the room.

My grandmother held my hands and said, "You look like your mom when she was your age." Then she stood up as well and quietly left the room.

I didn't move from my seat. I heard the sound of the car leaving and stared blankly at the door; their coldness had stunned me. In my dreams they had drawn me into their arms and taken me to their cozy house. Why were they so angry with me? Did they think I killed my mom? Did they also see me as a little troublemaker?

Our first meeting had lasted less than one hour. They didn't come again.

And so the orphanage turned out to be my second home. I later learned that my grandparents had denied any connection to me and had taken away my photos, even my sister's favorite. They claimed that their daughter and granddaughter had passed away ten years before. I decided to forget the day I saw my mother's parents. I decided I had just one grandfather and grandmother in my life. My pillow was often soaked with tears; I longed to see my sister and play our old games. The mountains gave us no food and bitter cold, but I longed for them just the same.

After the meeting with my mother's parents, men in dark suits came to the orphanage several times and asked me whether I remembered anything of my past and how I got so lost. My answer was always the same: "I don't remember." I was afraid any comments I made about my sister or grandparents would cause hurt to them.

I became one of the orphans, living at the orphanage and attending the school. The director of the orphanage decided to take care of me. Sometimes she gazed at me for a moment and patted my shoulder, but she never asked me about my past. I began to thrive, in my new home. In fact, it didn't take long for me to become the orphanage jump-rope champion.

"This is your schedule."

Teacher Song—as the sharp-eyed woman ordered me to

call her—threw a piece of paper onto the desk as soon as I stepped into her office. Forgetting I had planned to thank her for choosing me to join her dance group, I picked it up with haste. She wore a white shirt and black pants over her firm body. I looked around her office and saw that everything was in perfect order. In addition to Kim Il Sung's big picture in the center of the room, there were several pictures of a woman dancing. I assumed it was Teacher Song—it was hard to tell because of the thick makeup she wore in the pictures—but her body seemed unchanged. One bookcase was filled with books and the other with medals of various sizes.

"All the students get the same training. So don't say it's too much."

I was excited to learn something new. The schedule promised I would be busy, though I couldn't understand what a lot of the classes entailed.

"Of course not. Thanks for giving me this chance." I smiled at her, but she never smiled at me. Perhaps she didn't show her gentle face to anyone.

She asked, "Did you see your room?"

"Yes," I said, nodding my head, holding the paper with both hands. I had just come from my new room. It was for 20 girls, but I hadn't seen my roommates yet. The driver who'd picked me up from the orphanage said they were in the gymnasium all day and wouldn't be back until dinner.

"You'll stay there until the festival is over," she said. That room is for professional dancers, not amateurs like the children in other dancing groups, so try to learn from them and get along." Teacher Song stretched constantly as she spoke to me. It seemed that she couldn't stand to stay in one place.

"The big festival is exactly one year away, and we are preparing several performances for it. You are already several months behind the other dancers, but I believe you'll catch up. You'll get extra training after dinner every night. Got it?" She stretched her leg in my direction, leaning on the edge of the desk.

"Yes, I'll do my best." I was still anxious in her presence.

"Okay. You may go." As soon as she finished speaking, she sat down in her chair and turned to the papers on her desk. Just as I was leaving, she said, "Oh, by the way, don't mention that you're from the orphanage to the other dancers. Just say you were raised by your grandparents, who were in the army, if they ask."

She didn't look up at me as she spoke. I bowed and tiptoed out.

My new home was huge: several buildings, all much more colorful than the orphanage. All the furniture was new, too. The driver had told me most of the buildings were dormitories for the dancers. Next to them was a big, round gymnasium; I could hear music inside even from far away.

On the way there, I noticed several buildings under construction in the middle of the city: much had changed since the orphanage's sightseeing trip the previous year. I had lived in Pyongyang for ten years, but I still felt like a stranger there.

From the next day forward, I woke up at 5:30 A.M. and had breakfast in a huge cafeteria on the first floor of the dormitory at 6:00. In the gymnasium, 300 performers sang and danced all day, under the intense direction of Teacher Song. Megaphone in hand, she shouted at us from a balcony where she ran back and forth. Whenever someone made a mistake, she scolded her from above. Her booming voice kept us nervous and alert.

My name was the most famous among the dancers; Teacher Song enjoyed driving me hard. I always hoped someone else would come to instruct me, but it was always she who showed up for my private lesson after dinner. I couldn't believe she was over fifty; her body was elastic and tireless. Eventually, she stopped pointing and reprimanding me in front of the other students, but she didn't stop the private training until I was finally selected as one of the eleven dancers for one of the festival's main dancing performances, entitled "Unity." It supported the festival's theme, "For Anti-Imperialist Solidarity, Peace, and Friendship." Teacher Song wanted to express the goals of the festival through our dance.

The number eleven is meant to symbolize the five oceans and six continents, and in the Unity dance, five men and six women wore different-colored clothes, designed by Teacher Song. Each of us would wave a silk cloth, followed by a flag, and then a farm implement. We struggled with this routine in the beginning: Teacher Song demanded big, wild motions, and a different facial expression for each motion. We were instructed to wrap others in our cloths, and then wrap ourselves. Our struggle ended with the emergence of a boy in a uniform. We surrounded him and danced around him. We were unified through him: there would be no struggle, no further conflicts. I also took part in two other performances, the fan dance and the flag dance.

Teacher Song changed the choreography constantly; she never wanted us to be still. She continually emphasized that 177 countries had promised to participate in the festival.

"One single mistake would humiliate our country," she said. This was her favorite threat.

I went to bed utterly worn-out every night, but I felt alive. I felt as though there was a place for me.

My 19 roommates and I so looked forward to seeing the many people from other countries. We had to study a booklet titled *100 Questions and Answers for Foreigners*, and memorize all 100 to pass a test. We always carried a small book of Russian and English words in order to memorize them during our breaks. We had to be ready to welcome our guests, to help them understand our country, our lives, and the Great Leader.

My roommates and I were all selected for the fan dance. They were especially trained for traditional dance and all aspired to be professional traditional Korean dancers.

One day, Jangmi, after returning from a visit home, took a small yellow bottle out of her backpack. Sora, who usually slept next to her, instantly snatched it from her hand. "What is this?"

Jangmi closed her backpack and motioned for Sora to smell her hair, moving closer to Sora's nostrils.

"You smell so good!" Sora exclaimed, sniffing at Jangmi's neck. The rest of us surrounded them at once.

Jangmi gave each girl a whiff of her hair. "My mom bought it for me in a department store. It's *shampoo*. It came from abroad," she said, smiling exultantly.

"What? Shampoo? Is it soap? Why is it in your hair?"

"This kind of soap is specifically for your hair."

"You can't use it to wash other parts, body and face?"

We moved our noses close to smell the bottle.

"No, just for hair. It makes it feel like *velvet*," she cooed.

"Let me see." Not satisfied with the smell, several girls tried to touch the bottle.

"Be careful," she said, staring nervously at the other girls.

That night, they all made urgent calls to their parents and soon got their own bottles of shampoo. Except me, of course.

On the first of July, 1989, all the dancers were aflutter. Everyone was talking about the World Festival of Youth and Students. TV and radio broadcasters proclaimed its importance and repeated that only a powerful nation could host such a massive festival. We were proud of our country, and respect for our leader grew stronger. The festival opened with a young flush-faced woman and a man lighting a ceremonial torch, installed on the roof of the May Day Stadium for that night. I had never witnessed such a beautiful scene: every street was lit up, and we easily forgot the fatigue of our ceaseless rehearsals. It was fascinating to meet so many different kinds of people.

The performances we had devoted our lives to for a solid year succeeded in capturing the attention of foreigners. When I received a thunderous round of applause as I stood onstage, I felt my life had finally begun.

We were asked to attend the dancing festivals on Restoration Street for several nights, and that was where we first saw foreigners up close. Their dancing didn't have any rules, it seemed; they just shook their bodies and moved their arms and legs freely, with no sense of order. Watching them made me sweat. When they asked us to dance, we were at a loss for what to do. Without strict training, we didn't know how to move to the strange musical accompaniment.

The festival felt unreal, completely disconnected from our regular lives. We spent much of the time shouting for joy. When the Great Leader showed up on his special platform, we cried out, waving the flags; his appearance swept us off our feet. His image was so familiar—from my grandparents' house at the political offenders' camp to every wall at the orphanage and at the gymnasium, his picture had always followed me. When I had first seen his picture in the orphanage, identical to the one at my grandparents' house, I had felt a certain attachment to it, but fear as well. It seemed that he was watching over everything that had happened to me, and that he must have known about my past. And now he was standing in front of me! I broke down. But I don't know why the people around me were crying as well.

He was a part of my life. I had no way to choose otherwise.

It all passed so quickly. Although the festival ended and the foreigners went home, I carried its joy with me, right to the day that Teacher Song called me to her office. On the last day of the festival, Teacher Song was dancing, jumping around and embracing us, like a tiny, ebullient girl.

A few days later, I opened the brown door to her office with a big smile still on my face. "Teacher Song, did you call me?"

I found her sitting on the desk and talking on the phone, her face distorted. "Why is it impossible?" she demanded.

I immediately erased my grin. Slamming the phone down in a rage, she stood; the strict teacher had returned. Her eyes drifted to a picture on the wall of her playing the girl's role in *Girl Selling Flowers*. In the picture, she looked much younger than me; she was captured in profile, and the angle highlighted a deep dimple on her cheek. I could imagine her at that age. Nobody dared compete with her passion for dancing.

"Jia, you accomplished your task as well as I expected." She turned to me and gave a slight, tender smile. She never complimented any student: finally, she had recognized me! I was full of glee.

Teacher Song sat down on the ugly black sofa and winked at me to have a seat before her. It was the first time I'd seen her use the sofa. Cupping her chin in her hands and leaning her elbows on her knees, she looked small.

"The festival is over. As I said a year ago, you have to find another place to stay now. This place will be closed for a while. I tried to put you in a professional university, but it was 'impossible.' You're supposed to go back to the orphanage and wait there until your next home is decided upon. Do you want to go back?" she asked quietly.

My head was reeling. The end of the festival meant the end of my life. I shook my head. "I don't want to go back to the orphanage!" I cried. All I would do there is take care of kids and cook. To readjust to that life would be too hard—my mind was already far away.

Teacher Song sighed. "Go back to your room, Jia. Let's figure out what we can do. I'll file a report with the Party on your achievements in this festival and call you later. But pack your things anyway."

Despite her reputation, I had become unafraid of Teacher Song. She had devoted her life to dancing and was the most passionate person I had ever met. I wanted to stay with her. There was still so much more to learn from her.

I went back to my room, dejected. The others were restless, halfheartedly packing their things, waiting for their parents to pick them up and talking about their new universities. I sneaked out of the room and sat down on the stairs at the end of the hall. This year had been like a dream that passed too quickly. I felt as if my life had skipped from my childhood on the mountain to the present. I had changed: my arms and legs were much longer; my shirts and pants didn't cover my limbs. I could hear my heart beating. The more I thought about the orphanage, the more pain I felt. I remembered how happy the director of the orphanage had been when I left to dance under Teacher Song! How strongly she had encouraged me never to return! To go back to that dead world now was more than I could contemplate.

My roommates left, one by one. The building, once boisterous, became as quiet as a mausoleum, and I paced the halls like a restless spirit. At last, I packed my things and waited for the call from Teacher Song. I knew my mother's parents would not help me, if they remembered me at all. I blamed myself for thinking about them at that moment.

Several days later, Teacher Song stopped by my room. Leaning against the door, she spoke in a soft voice. "You don't have many choices. The orphanage said they would welcome you if you like to go back."

I held my backpack tightly to my chest and looked at her with despair. I wanted to say that I would do anything to stay, perform any task.

Teacher Song moved close to me and put her hand on my shoulder. "I asked one of my friends, a government official, to give you a new job, and she found a good place. You can dance over there, too. I didn't have time to discuss it with you because I had to answer right away. If you'll take it, we have to leave right now."

Teacher Song carried my backpack and I followed her,

my face glowing with joy. As we walked, side by side, she held my hand and said, "It won't be so bad there—you can dance and sing and see how professional dancers live. They'll give you your own house soon, and enough rations, too. But it'll be a tiring job. I'll try to find a better one for you, but for now I have no choice but to follow the order from above. Let's see what happens." Her hand felt warm and strange. She had been so harsh and cold, always scaring the students. Her head was full of dance steps. We never had time to get to know her or talk to her outside of class. How could I ever thank her enough for opening the door to the real world for me.

When I climbed into the dark-brown van, already waiting for me in front of the building, she let go of my hand. I looked up at her with tearful eyes and gave her a letter I had written. She looked down at the letter and was silent, her eyes filling with tears. I hadn't expected her to cry for me, but her tears didn't stop flowing.

She spoke slowly, without wiping her cheeks. "If your mother had seen your performance, she would have been so happy. She was the best student I've ever had and you inherited her talent, Jia. When I first saw you on the stage at the orphanage, I knew who you were. I thought my favorite student had returned to me."

As we drove off, I watched her with widened eyes, trying to keep her in sight, craning my neck as her figure grew smaller and smaller. I didn't understand why my life couldn't be my own, why there was always a chain, emerging from deep in the past, stretching into the present, that bound me to my fate.

5

Into a Different World

Thirty minutes later, the van deposited me in front of a tall, imposing building, my bag at my heels. The driver shouted at a young man in a blue uniform standing erect outside the glass doors. My gaze followed the building up to the sky. Two brown towers, like giant chopsticks, pressed down on me. They looked like separate buildings but were connected in the middle by a tunnel, like a bridge across a river.

The Kaya Hotel was the one of the biggest hotels in Pyongyang. Foreign guests stayed there during the 1989 festival. The building was visible from Rŭngra Island, where I had stayed with other dancers during the festival, but I had never seen it up close.

I gasped in amazement. *Is this where I'm supposed to be?*

The young uniformed man stepped into my line of sight,

and I knew I had to follow him. When I turned around, the van had already disappeared.

Inside, the vast interior of the lobby spread out before me. Everyone seemed to be staring at me. I kept my head down and chased after the uniformed man. Turning left off the main hall, we arrived at an open door, and he gestured for me to go in.

Stepping inside, I found myself in an auditorium, on the shining, hard, wooden stage. Glancing around the interior, my eyes were drawn to two women, who stopped talking and looked at me.

"Come here," the younger woman commanded me, her high-pitched voice reverberating through the room. "You'll share a room with Aunt Ann. She'll show you around." With her chin she pointed to the woman at her side. She continued, speaking quickly, "You'll be on standby for our dancing group—I've heard a lot about you from Teacher Song. I'll introduce you to the other dancers when they arrive tomorrow morning. You can't participate in the performances yet—you're the youngest and a novice. I wasn't expecting you, actually, I just got the call from Teacher Song. Learn a lot from the other dancers and you can assist them for the time being."

Everything about this commanding woman was simple. Her bobbed hair, hanging like a curtain above her shoulders, was pitch-black and glossy. Her black skirt and jacket looked worn-out compared to her shiny hair. As she spoke, she flipped her hair behind her right ear. Her eyes, nose, and mouth were positioned appropriately on her face, and everything was the correct size. Her hands, however, were disproportionately large; they were too big and sturdy-looking.

"Aunt Ann, take her to your room and instruct her as we just discussed," the woman said, turning to the older woman beside her, who appeared to be in her 50s. Aunt Ann looked up at us, nodding her head.

The commanding woman glanced impetuously at her wristwatch and grabbed her hefty gray bag. The tendons on the back of her hand jumped out. "I'll come back tomorrow. Be back here at eight A.M. See you then."

As she spun around to leave, she stumbled, and my hands reached toward her involuntarily to prevent her from falling. She straightened suddenly, turned back to me, and said, "Oh, call me Director Park. Make yourself at home. Teacher Song was also my teacher." She slipped through the door. Her exit was as sudden as her introduction.

After she left, I had a chance to look around the auditorium. The stage was medium-sized, a little bigger than the one at the orphanage. But the auditorium was beautiful and clean, with about a hundred deep-red seats. They looked comfortable. A thick curtain of red velvet hung at the back of the stage.

"This is the small stage. There's a much bigger one downstairs, but they don't open it very often; most of the time the dancers practice here." I turned and found Aunt Ann standing behind me, wearing a round khaki hat and a simple uniform. Covered in ivory cotton work gloves, her hands looked bigger than the rest of her body. Her half-moon eyes disappeared when she smiled.

"This building is huge," I said, glancing around the theater.

She took off her gloves. "And you've only seen a tiny part of it. Let's go. I'll take you to our room. We will be roommates from today on." She looked down at my backpack, next to my feet, and grinned. "Compared to this place, our room is tiny. If that backpack is all you brought, that's just fine." She stuffed her gloves in the small pocket of her jacket.

I followed Aunt Ann through the lobby, and at length into the hotel's cafeteria. Six shimmering chandeliers dangled from the ivory ceiling. A fragrant aroma pierced the air, and I wondered what food they were cooking; it was different from the aroma of regular food. I looked around, but there were no dishes on the tables.

"What is this smell, Aunt Ann? It's incredibly good."

"Yes, right. The smell is—it's not the food. It's the tea the foreigners drink every day, instead of water. You're right, the aroma is good, but the taste is so bad...so bitter. It's like tea from hell." She moved as close as possible to me and said under her breath, "I stole a taste once when I had to clean up the tables. I was nervous other people might see, so I poured the rest of a cup into my mouth. *Blech*—I rushed to the restroom and rinsed out my mouth over and over."

I couldn't believe that such a sweet smell came with a bitter flavor.

When we passed through the kitchen, people wearing white from top to bottom stopped their chores. "Hey, Ann, is she the new girl?" they asked. I bobbed my head toward them. They chuckled and said, "You're lucky to have such a nice old roommate."

Aunt Ann put her hands on her waist and shouted at them, "Who says I'm old? I'm young enough to be her friend."

People laughed. "Oh, well, if you say so..." They all seemed so pleasant.

Continuing down a long hall, we reached our room. Aunt Ann opened the door. At first sight, the room looked about the same size as a toilet. I couldn't help comparing it to my previous room, which I had shared with nineteen girls.

Aunt Ann had everything organized so well. "You can put your things on the right side," she said. "Fortunately, I don't own a lot, either."

Two jackets, a skirt, a pair of pants, and several perfectly ironed shirts hung evenly on the wall. Her things looked simple. On the windowsill, there was an old radio, with a long antenna sticking up from the side. Through the window I could see the Taedong River in the distance; the room had a good view of Pyongyang. In one corner, two books and a little, transparent, chipped cup sat atop a miniature tea table.

"Do you live here?" I asked, putting my backpack down where Aunt Ann indicated. I thought she must have a separate house in the city where she could go to see her family.

"This building has been my home since I lost my whole family five years ago." She took off her hat, revealing a head of long, shocking white hair, tied neatly with a black string. Her unwrinkled skin didn't match her hair at all.

"What happened?" The question came out unexpectedly, and I realized immediately I shouldn't have asked it. Feeling ill at ease, I studied her face.

"There was a fire in a factory five years ago. My husband and son worked there together, but one day, they didn't come home for dinner. I waited and waited for them. After a while, I heard from my neighbors about the accident. So…that's the story," she said, folding her hat and gloves neatly and placing them on the tea table.

"Oh, I'm so sorry." I was embarrassed to have drawn out such a sad story.

"It's okay. It's history. My sadness has dried out, and I'm

sure they must have better lives in the other world. They're always happy in my dreams. They never cry... Never say they miss me... I decided not to drive myself crazy thinking about them." She smiled widely at me. "I never expected such a young girl for a roommate. Are you twenty yet?"

"I'm eighteen."

"I can't even remember being that age. What was I like back then, I wonder. Was I pretty like you?" She seemed transported for the briefest moment, and then came back to me. "You're lucky to be here—everyone at the hotel is nice."

I looked at her and said with a grin, "Yes, I think you're right."

I thought about Teacher Song. How considerate she was! She must have toiled hard to send me to such a good place.

From the next day forward, I was one of the busiest people in the hotel. In the early morning, before the dancers and singers came to the practice room, I had to clean it up. They were professional dancers and singers for guests at the hotel, and they practiced every day to stay on top of the game. They were carefully selected to work at the hotel and justifiably proud of their status. In addition to performing traditional drum and fan dances wearing *hanbok* and revolutionary dances wearing military uniforms, they could all play at least two musical instruments, and they were talented singers as well.

Running errands for Director Park and helping with Aunt Ann's chores were also my duties. As soon as Director Park introduced me to the other dancers, I had to learn how to assist them and to find out where their things belonged, like cosmetics and costumes.

There were 50 in the group, the most fashionable women I had ever seen. They even played the male roles in the dances and operas, so their vocal ranges were impressively wide. I was excited to meet real, professional dancers. Every morning, they practiced how to smile and gesture. I never thought a day could be so short.

One day, Director Park beckoned me over as I was gazing enviously at the dancers practicing onstage. "Jia, come here."

I rushed to her. "Yes, Director Park?" Although she looked frail and girlish, she was severe, make no mistake, and she didn't tolerate laziness in her dancers. Sometimes I couldn't help smiling, because her teaching style and hard facial expressions reminded me so much of Teacher Song.

"Jia, this woman will teach you to dance from now on. Call her Teacher Son." A young woman was walking toward us—Sunyoung, one of the best dancers at the hotel. She always wore a bright smile.

Sunyoung's high, sonorous voice echoed through the practice room. "See, Teacher, look at her long legs and arms, they'll help her make much prettier gestures than anyone else here." She stood next to me and said with a low voice, so Director Park couldn't hear, "If you don't mind, just call me Sister; I'm hardly old enough to be called a teacher."

Sunyoung's face attracted attention. The first time I saw her among the dancing team members, I felt she must be from another country. She was the tallest of the group, and her nose started prominently from her forehead, while her thick, folded eyelids gave her features a clear-cut look. After that first meeting, we became best friends.

The dancers who worked at the hotel thought I was an orphan from a good family who was only there for practical training. They were all from families with good back-grounds, and their lives were as splendid as their appear-ance; it seemed they could get anything they wanted. After the festival, having curly hair became popular in Pyong-yang, and women bought colorful blouses and skirts from other countries at import markets. Only a chosen few, such as these dancers, could afford those fashions.

Employees were chosen to work at the hotel only after passing an investigation into their family background. The stigma of belonging to the "reactionary class," or to the "commonly" or "extremely" bad, or having any other blem-ish on one's family record meant immediate disqualification. The dancers were proud of having made the cut, and they assumed I, too, came from a privileged background. When I started working in the souvenir section as a clerk, the dancers and other employees expressed sympathy at my having been assigned extra work. I had to practice dancing after my shift at the souvenir section, or at night with Sunyoung. Some dancers envied my job as a clerk and complained that they couldn't take on extra work because their families would lose face.

"The souvenir section's the best place to see foreigners up close and have private conversations with them," they would say.

As a matter of fact, I didn't mind doing the extra work, if only as a token of gratitude to the hotel for accepting me. I wanted also to make up for 15 years of isolation from the real world.

Three years after my arrival, the hotel provided me with a flat nearby. It had been allocated for an employee of the hotel, but nobody else had wanted to move into such a small space. Finally, I would be on own in the city.

My determination to move was sparked, in time, by Sunyoung's tragedy.

A year and a half after we became friends, gossip about Sunyoung started brewing among the dancers.

"She's a slut."

I'll never forget the shock of hearing that word spat out by the other dancers. They avoided talking about it with me because they knew Sunyoung and I were always together. I began to notice, however, that whenever we showed up in the practice room, the usual babble of voices would halt. I worried about whether Sunyoung had heard the rumors, but she was the same woman: full of vitality, gay, constantly joking; she got along with others very well. I felt the other dancers were secretly jealous of her, and I could only hope the rumor would die out.

After a month of continual performances, the dancers had their first break in a long while.

That morning, no one was in the practice hall. I rolled up my sleeves and started cleaning the mirrors of a dressing room, when Sister Min and Sister Oh came in. Min exclaimed, "Sure, no smoke without fire! She did it. It's obvious. Otherwise, those kinds of dirty stories wouldn't follow Sunyoung around. How could she do that? So gross…. Such a wanton woman!"

When they discovered me, they were startled and shut their mouths right away.

I pretended I'd heard nothing. "Good morning, sisters."

"Hi, Jia."

They sat at the dressing table, looking at their faces in the mirror. "My skin is getting drier. I hate winter," Sister Oh said, feigning innocence. I organized the scattered cosmetics.

"Have you heard the gossip?" I asked, not looking at them.

Sister Oh, who always enjoyed a good rumor, turned to me. "About what?" she asked.

The mention of a story got them excited. I kept my head down and continued, "About Sister Sunyoung... Can you believe it?" I pretended to know.

"See? Even she's heard!" Sister Oh shouted with joy, and the two women dragged their chairs over to me.

Sister Min grabbed my right arm. "What did you hear? Is there more recent news?"

"No, not really... You know... I wonder if Sister Sunyoung has heard; she wouldn't do those things anymore if she had ears."

"Exactly! How dare she give her body away? Isn't she scared? I heard that foreign men are different from ours. Look at them: so big and tall. Actually she's big and tall compared to us, so maybe it's possible for her." They giggled, covering their mouths with their hands.

I felt flushed. "But do you think it's true? It might just be gossip. I can't imagine..."

Sister Oh stood up and leaned against the dressing table, forcing me to stop cleaning. Her face was red with excitement, her nostrils flaring. "No, Jia. I thought like that when I first heard, but Guard Kim confirmed it yesterday. He knows all the gossip here, and everything he says turns out to be true. He told me that Sunyoung and Guard Lee have worked out their dirty strategy. While she and their foreign target are doing it in the room, Guard Lee sneaks in, takes pictures, and threatens to notify the target's country and the hotel of what he saw, unless he's paid in US dollars. After that, Sunyoung and Guard Lee share the money."

She waved her hand in front of her mouth. "Ugh, I'm making my mouth dirty. But it seems like it's true. Guard Kim said that while guards were drinking together, Guard Lee boasted about how he made money. Isn't it weird?"

Sister Oh sat down in front of the dressing table again and took a good look at her face. "I really need some good cream…. Jia, I understand how you're feeling now. You follow her like a real sister. You must be so shocked. To be honest, I thought you already knew. We even suspected you were part of her scheme. Anyway…I'm glad you're not. I really respected her when I first came here. She was my ideal. But now I feel ashamed for having looked up to such a dust rag."

I ran all over the hotel looking for Sunyoung. What was going on? I didn't believe it. I wouldn't believe it until I heard it from Sunyoung directly. But she was nowhere to be found.

My last stop was the restaurant, where I found her chatting gaily with Cook Kim. I could hear her high-pitched laughter from across the room. How happy she was! How elegant she looked! I felt determined to stop the dirty gossip about her at once.

I approached her and tugged on her hand. She looked at my sweaty face with startled eyes, and asked in alarm, "What's wrong? What's wrong with you, Jia? Has something happened?"

I dragged her from the kitchen, forgetting to excuse myself to Cook Kim. We went to a restroom, and I checked under the door of each stall for shoes. Finding nobody, I turned to her and hissed, "Sister Sunyoung, do you know you're the topic of the most horrible gossip right now? Have you heard the thumping lies being told about you? I want to hear from you directly that it's not true. Tell them it's not true. Stop their tongues!" I looked into her eyes, pleading, but could read nothing in her face. "Sister Sunyoung, please say something."

Sunyoung's face had darkened. "I have no choice but to do it, Jia," she groaned.

"Jia. The gossip is right. Of course, it is more complicated and they exaggerate. But mostly, it's right."

I stepped back and tried to still my reeling head.

"Jia... I don't know how to begin telling this story. I wanted to tell you about it, but I didn't know where to start. I'm not the slut people say I am." She looked at my neck, not at my eyes.

"Several years ago, I fell in love with a foreigner. I knew it was forbidden. I never thought it would happen to me. He lived here as a student and officer in the consulate of his country, and would often attend my performances. When I went home every night, he would be waiting at the gate of the hotel with a smile and a flower. At first, he couldn't speak Korean very well. Of course, I was scared of him, but also curious; I didn't shun him. After a month of flowers, I got used to seeing him and was able to meet his eyes with confidence. He was beautiful. I liked his gray eyes and dark-blond hair. Gradually he began speaking to me in broken Korean. You can't imagine how cute that was. I had never heard the beating of my heart inside me before, but it happened whenever I saw him. We secretly started going out. Jia, try to understand, the rules didn't matter anymore. I danced for him.... I laughed, thinking of him."

Her smile was darkening into a frown.

"We did what we shouldn't do. I wanted to express my feelings and accept him, not just in my heart. Who cared about finding a man with stable status and power for the future? I didn't want to control my feelings. That was the happiest time of my life, but one day screwed up everything." Sunyoung studied my face for a second, but my eyes never left hers.

"When we were in bed in his room, Guard Lee sneaked inside and took pictures of us. He had suspected our relationship and threatened to notify the hotel and the embassy. We were freaked out—I begged Guard Lee, but, what was worse, he recorded our conversation, and demanded a lot of money. Above all, I was worried about my lover; he was more scared than me. He called his parents instantly to send the money, and as soon as he got it, he gave it to Guard Lee and went back to his country, telling the embassy he was ill and homesick. He left without a word to me. I couldn't believe it. After he'd gone, I was out of my mind. I knocked on his door so many times, but his room was empty. I even thought about killing myself. I cried while holding a razor blade to cut my wrist in the restroom. His leaving didn't make things simpler; Guard Lee kept the tape recorder and the pictures and said he would give the evidence to the hotel unless I took other foreigners to bed. He directed me to entice foreigners and play out the same scenario. He didn't let me lock the door while I did the job. He would come into the room and threaten the target. He took money from those pathetic victims."

Sunyoung paused, and I watched her face. I had never seen her so tired. Her long lashes made shadows under her eyes.

"You don't know how humiliating it was, but there was no way I could avoid him or run away. Sometimes he brought the foreigners to me. After a while, I stopped caring; my heart had melted." Sunyoung rubbed her face with her hands. "I want out of this nightmare. I haven't followed his orders very well recently. He is angry with me and criticizes my laziness. I thought he would make enough money and leave me alone. I implored him so many times, and he seemed to feel pity for me. I thought if I persuaded him, I never imagined he would tell other people." Sunyoung broke into tears and covered her whole face with both hands, as though she was trying to hide the painful life she had led.

My hatred for the people spreading rumors about Sunyoung expanded like a balloon. I couldn't offer her any comfort, I couldn't say a word. I was a useless friend.

I suggested we get the tape recorder and pictures from Guard Lee by any means. We thought he might keep them in the room he shared with Janitor Lee, who was a close friend of Aunt Ann's. That was as far as we got that day.

Sunyoung was relieved. "Oh, Jia, this has taken over my entire life. I feel I have gotten old fast over the past few years. I sleep, but I can't sleep. I wake up in the middle of the night and stare at the wall until morning comes. I really need to resolve this."

I spent a sleepless night plotting solutions; I even considered killing Guard Lee. Was he human? No. What could I do for Sunyoung? I needed to protect her at all cost.

The next day, I rushed to the practice room. I had overslept. The dancers were gabbing quietly. They hadn't begun rehearsing yet. Director Park wasn't there either.

"Good morning, sisters," I said, to no one in particular. "What is going on?"

"Director Park just left with Sunyoung," Sister Min said.

"What happened? Why did they leave together?"

"Sunyoung was just turned in to the police for prostitution and for blackmail with Guard Lee. Director Park didn't believe it, and followed the police; I have never seen her so desperate. Think about it, she lavished such care on Sunyoung. She was the only one who didn't know Sunyoung was a prostitute. Ha! With such a pure face and a radiant smile all the time, who could have imagined? She tricked all of us and disgraced our dancing group. She deserves to be executed."

Sister Oh spoke up with a bang, "Do you remember what I said, Jia? The gossip Guard Kim heard from Guard Lee on that night of drinking? It wasn't just Guard Kim who heard, someone who was there reported it to the hotel. The intelligence bureau investigated Guard Lee's room and found the evidence. They took Guard Lee yesterday night and Sunyoung early this morning."

I was stunned. All I could hear after that was the low hum of voices.

That afternoon, Director Park returned with sloping shoulders. I tried to ask about Sunyoung, but she only murmured, "You'll have a new teacher as of tomorrow." Then she went to her office and didn't come out for the rest of the day.

Several days later, I heard that Sunyoung was sentenced to life in prison and that Guard Lee was scheduled to be executed. That was all anyone heard. Their names were never to be mentioned again—that was the strict order from the hotel manager at the morning meeting. I wouldn't see Sunyoung again in this life.

In the late spring and early summer, the dancers and officers sometimes went out on weekends for recreation. It was a mid-June morning when a group of us took the hotel bus for the annual trip to Mt. Taesŏng Resort. The bus drove through hills for the better part of an hour, and out the window we saw grazing deer and the waterfall on Lake Mich'ŏn. As usual, we first stopped at the Revolutionary Patriot Memorial on the mountain in order to pay tribute to national heroes. It was my fourth visit to the memorial since I'd joined the hotel, but the imposing red granite busts of the martyrs still frightened me.

Arriving at the resort, we saw that several couples were having wedding pictures taken. One bride wore a purple *hanbok* with white azalea flowers spread all over the skirt. She posed with a big smile, holding her husband's left arm tightly. He had a small build, and the wide skirt of her *hanbok* overwhelmed him.

"Wow, their first child will be a girl," Youngmi snapped, as we looked at that couple from the bus.

"How do you know?" I asked.

"Haven't you heard that if the bride smiles on the wedding day, the couple will have a daughter? Look at her! They'll have a dozen daughters." She pouted, her lower lip sticking out slightly.

"But on a day of celebration, smiling looks much better than a serious face." I wasn't buying it.

We watched them jealously for a while. The weather was good, and people walked, smiled, and played games in groups everywhere. It was on that day that I first met Seung-gyu. He was a friend of Jongmu, the hotel manager's son.

As soon as we got off the bus, we sat down on an empty patch of grass and opened our lunch box, prepared by Cook Kim at 5 A.M. According to his logic, people like us, who use our knees and jump around all the time, should eat plenty of protein. His main dishes always contained small anchovies, black beans, and egg roll with rice and *kimchi*.

"Does he think we'll jump around today too?"

The dancers grumbled about Cook Kim's lunch. Most of them hated anchovies because you could see their eyes.

"Jia, here you go."

I finished off my anchovies at every meal, so the others called me "anchovy girl" and often gave me theirs. I liked Cook Kim's way of frying them with sugar and millet jelly; they were crispy, like a snack. My grandmother would cook them that way, and my sister and I quarreled over who could eat more.

We had almost finished the lunch when Jongmu and Seunggyu came and joined us.

"Why did you guys wear your military uniforms? You're screwing up the relaxing atmosphere," the oldest dancer, Myungha, said, poking fun. Jongmu, a soldier, was like a member of our family. He always boasted that he was the only male dancer and that he had to take care of more than 50 women.

"We had an unexpected training program. You should appreciate it—people will assume we're bodyguards, protecting the pretty women."

"Then don't sit down next to us, stand up and concentrate on your duty," Myungha teased.

"Oh, not you, sister. You don't need our protection; no one would want you."

"You birdbrain—" She shook her head and we all laughed.

"By the way, this is my friend, Seunggyu," Jongmu said. "We train together, so I dragged him here." Jongmu patted his friend's back and gave me a smile. I knew Seunggyu by sight; I had run into him several times in the hallways behind the stage.

Seunggyu just nodded his head slightly. A dapper figure, he had big eyes, like a cow, with long eyelashes and no eyelids. I couldn't believe such a pretty face could endure military training.

We sang and danced casually; some dancers tried to copy the moves of others, and the laughter and chatting never stopped. Director Park brought her husband, who looked much older than she, and their daughter. As a couple, they looked more like father and daughter; his good smile and humor must have attracted her.

"I brought *paduk*. Let's play," Director Park's husband, Sangwoo, said. He took the folded *paduk* board and two small jars with black and white pieces out of his big backpack. He proudly unfolded the board. "I bought this one when I went to China. It's portable. So convenient!"

Seunggyu stood up and said, "That's for old people. It's a waste of time. You comrades go ahead, but think about it: we're outside to enjoy the sun and fresh air, not to stare at a small square board." He seemed to be talking in my direction, and, dusting off his backside, he suddenly fixed his eyes on me. "Hey. Let's go on some rides." He smoothed his crinkled uniform.

I looked around at the others and back at him again, but his eyes didn't move. Sangwoo said, smirking, "Jia, he is asking you out. You shouldn't turn him down, he'll lose face." People chuckled.

Seunggyu blushed up to the tips of his ears and shot a fiery glance at Sangwoo. "She's the only one who looks active. That's all. That's why I'm asking her." His face reminded me of a red carrot. "Are you coming or not? If you want to go, let's go right now before more people rush over there."

We went on the rides and walked around the zoo, the fountain, and the botanical garden. It had been announced that outdoor swimming would not begin until the next weekend, but the area was already packed with people. It was difficult to enjoy those places in a crowd, and I was tired of walking and standing in long lines.

Seunggyu wasn't very talkative. "I've seen your performances several times," he said finally.

I looked at him with wide eyes, but he was watching some wolves, lazily napping in their cage.

When we got back to the grass, the others were gone. I looked around and saw that the bus wasn't there either.

Seunggyu laughed. "Look! The old people left early to take a nap! Let's go back. I'll take you home."

The next day, when I showed up in the practice room, dancers rushed up to me in excitement and asked about what we did, where we went, and how Seunggyu treated me. I might as well have been an exotic animal at the zoo. I just joked with them, "Cook Kim was smart—he must have known I actually *would* use my legs a lot yesterday. All I remember is how much we walked."

They giggled. "You can take all of our anchovies at lunch today," one said. "We're sure he'll make them again for you."

After our day out, Seunggyu often came to my performances and waited to take me home. Having somebody wait for me gave me a warm feeling. Since Sunyoung's arrest, I had become more reserved. I no longer intended to open my heart to others. When each day's activities are all arranged for you, you simply wake up, go through the motions, and prepare for the next day; you don't have to think about anything else. I tried not to notice the emptiness growing inside me.

When Seunggyu came along, the road I had been walking alone was no longer empty. His confidence about life became mine as well.

At the hotel, I was happy, and there was nothing to worry about. Sunyoung's story was fading into the past. I danced for myself, striving to be as professional as the other dancers, and sometimes I even got the main part in a performance. After four years at the hotel, I had grown fond of everyone. It didn't take much effort to perform the same dances for guests and sell the same items at the souvenir shop. I practiced hard, every day. I was satisfied with everything around me and was becoming concerned only for myself.

On the way home at night, however, I began to notice changes. I could feel the light in the city dimming. After the death of our leader, Kim Il Sung, in July of 1994, most of our performances depicted sad stories. The sudden death of the Great Leader had shocked our country—there was a rumor that people had died from sorrow—but the tragedy was only the precursor of impending hardships. There were fewer and fewer performances at the hotel. People's faces were darkening as well. My neighbors were becoming reticent. Sometimes they mentioned in passing that their rations were decreasing; both the quantity and quality of what we were receiving were going downhill. Cereals mixed in with rice created digestive problems, and people started selling their household goods at markets to buy food. We wanted to talk to each other about the problems, but couldn't. All we heard from the government was: "Trust Kim Jong Il and the Party." Most of us did; we felt we had no choice.

When eight dancers didn't show up for work, the hotel manager said they had decided to devote their lives to being perfect mothers and wives, but everyone knew the hotel was simply cutting staff. The number of guests dwindled and the rules stiffened. The hotel manager warned us not to wear colorful clothes anymore. Curly hair was still acceptable, but we had to tie it back with thick elastics.

It took me a while to realize that despite my seeming freedom, I was still stuck in an isolated world. It was simply of a different design.

Several days of rain had turned everything in the city gray except the Kaesŏnmun (Arch of Triumph). I was standing before it with Seunggyu. My performance that day, meant to recognize an official's 40 years of military service, was canceled because several government officials, including the honoree, had to leave for the countryside in the morning. I asked Seunggyu to take me to the Kaesŏnmun because I thought its grandeur might cheer me up. At the foot of Moran Hill, I looked up at the largest arch in the world, with its 10,500 blocks of shiny white granite. But, against my expectations, it made me feel worse. Attempting to read the revolutionary hymn inscribed at the top made me nauseated. I didn't want to touch the white granite, I didn't want to feel its coldness.

"I'll be away for a couple of weeks, maybe more," Seunggyu said. He looked uncomfortable in his casual clothes.

Out of his uniform, he looked much younger than his 27 years; he could pass for a teenager. A pack of cigarettes stuck out of the chest pocket of his black jacket.

"Because of the flood?" I asked.

One year earlier, in 1995, the flood had been the main topic of conversation everywhere: so many were dead, houses and property had drifted away. Then, in July and August of 1996, another round of floods. Aunt Ann's province on the east coast had suffered the worst damage. She said that people there had their rations cut off entirely. Seunggyu and I walked away from the arch toward Moran Park.

"Do you have to command your platoon to assist this time too?"

Seunggyu snapped some branches from the tree next to him and grumbled, "I didn't join the army to drag dead bodies from the water." The year before, his platoon had been sent to collect corpses in the countryside, and he had confided that 70 percent of the land had been devastated by the two years of flooding. The army was worried about the possible spread of infectious diseases.

"But Seunggyu, that is also an important job for the people and the country. Think about it—we should be helping each other. Soldiers are helping—isn't that why everyone respects them?" I was trying to smooth his anger.

"Not for *those* people," he snapped. Seunggyu didn't like anything that cast shadows on his bright future. I felt sad and distant from him.

"Where are you going?" I asked.

"Who knows? I just follow orders. Maybe the mining regions—they got it the worst this time." His eyes glowed. "I'm wasting my time on useless vermin. We're no better than janitors—we just take away bigger trash than they do."

"What do you mean?" I looked at him as he flung a branch toward the pond with all his might.

"Jia, who lives in mines and isolated mountain villages? Trash, reactionary elements. Everyone knows we don't need these people in this society. We're just going there to throw trash away."

"You think they're not worthy of sleeping in a cemetery?" I tried to conceal my emotion. His eyes followed the branches as they fell on the pond.

"Jia, you don't know about those people. You haven't seen them, that's why you're generous to them. But I have: they are like zombies. They don't think, they just walk and eat."

I wasn't able to defend them, having left the mountain myself and hidden my early life. But, looking at Seunggyu's contemptuous profile, I was reminded of my maternal grandfather. "Don't say that. They're still human, they feel happiness and sadness like you do. How do you know what they think? Have you ever talked with them sincerely?" I was indignant.

"What's wrong with you, Jia? I'm talking about useless people. I have *seen* them; you haven't. Why are you so angry?" Seunggyu dusted off his hands and stepped toward me.

I lowered my head, trying to swallow the rage in my throat. "I'm sorry, I don't like hearing you talk with such contempt."

Seunggyu took my hand and shook it lightly. "Let's go. You are disappointed about the cancellation of the performance today. It'll be fine. I have never seen you mad like that, Jia. I know you have a good heart, but you should learn when to show it, and for whom."

There was no one on the street. The gloomy sky had

driven everyone away, and we headed to the subway, the pride of Pyongyang. For the festival in 1989, I had memorized an introduction to the subway system in Russian and English, to show off these underground palaces to our foreign visitors.

Kaesŏn Station had always been full of young couples going home after dates in Kaesŏn Youth Park, where the Great Leader, Kim Il Sung, made his first speech after liberation from the Japanese in 1945. But today the subway no longer seemed magnificent to me. I felt I was being sucked into the darkness pouring out of my heart.

6

The Limitations of Human Beings

One morning the following year, I had to stop at Saesal-lim Street on my way to the hotel, before crossing the Taedong River. Lines of people chained together marched past me, their heads hanging low. The policemen leading them shouted that they had committed crimes against the nation, and they had to walk around in public to demonstrate the consequences of their crimes.

Someone behind me whispered, "The line is getting longer. They ran away to China for food, but got caught. They'll be punished harshly. Oh, look at those little children." I turned back and saw two middle-aged women talking. As soon as our eyes met, they turned and left hastily.

By 1997, the country still had not recovered from the floods of the previous two years, and countless numbers had succumbed to cholera and paratyphoid fever. Seunggyu, observing the pile of dead bodies, said that it was impossible to count the dead. On TV and radio, the government told us the nation had recovered from the natural disasters, but the situation only seemed to be worsening. The appearance of the city had changed completely; instead of going to work, people wandered all day. The streets teemed with people carrying big bags on their shoulders, as they went into alleys to sell their belongings. The police couldn't control the black market. Never had street markets been so popular, nor the goods so various. Groups of people sitting on the sidewalks displaying their belongings had become fixtures in the residential areas. Houses were emptied, and the sellers far outnumbered the buyers.

Beyond downtown Pyongyang, across the Taedong River, I would often see groups of children in the street markets. These children were called *kkotjebi,* which means "flower swallows." Their name suggests lovely lives, but their lives consisted of watching other people eat. If someone didn't finish his or her food, the fastest *kkotjebi* would snatch the bowl and gulp down the leftovers. Sometimes, begging for food and money, they offered to sing and perform "black art." They called their performances black art because the performances might endanger their lives, but it was worth the risk.

I once saw a little boy boast of his talents in a loud voice as he grabbed the clothes of passersby. He insisted he could put needles through his ears, and some people stopped in their tracks to look at him. He produced two rusty, long needles and slid one through each ear, though his face didn't show any pain. When a young woman took a closer look, she cried out, "My God, look at them—his ears are covered with holes and scabs." All at once, the spectators pushed forward to look at his ears, then in consternation they left without giving him any money. Some women gave him bread or rice, out of compassion. The food seemed to satisfy him.

Walking through a street market to the hotel early one morning, I saw a small *kkotjebi* being dragged away by two policemen. He twisted with all his might to get out of their hands, wailing, "Sir, I'm not *kkotjebi!* I have parents waiting for me at home. I need to go back!"

The policeman holding his two legs under his arm snarled, "Cut it out, you stinky brat, I've been watching you for days." The other held the boy's neck at his waist, pressing it hard, until the boy's face turned red and he stopped resisting. His body looked like a small tree, carried between two men. No one in the market paid the slightest attention.

A familiar voice, shouting at the top of her lungs, caught my attention. She cried out at the people passing her food stall, "Three rolls for ten won! You can't find them cheaper!" A stain spread over the front of her grimy whitish shirt, attracting my gaze. She had been one of my teachers at the orphanage. She was nice to everyone; sometimes I even slept in her room. She had taught sex education to the girls when we gathered in her room—things we couldn't learn from other teachers. In those days, she was pretty, passionate, and determined to bridge the distance between teacher and student.

The year I left the orphanage, she moved to a small school outside Pyongyang. The other girls and I wrote a farewell letter and shed tears because we knew we'd never see her again. I couldn't have imagined I'd run into her in a street market; she had aged so much in just a few years.

"Excuse me, Teacher Oh?" Pushing through the passersby, I approached her and sized up her brown, oval face;

I was sure who it was when I saw the small mole under her lip. Teacher Oh fell silent; I thought perhaps she hadn't recognized me.

"Do you remember me, Teacher Oh?" I asked, getting closer to let her see my face.

She smiled. "How can I forget you? Little dancing girl..."

She grabbed my wrists and held them lightly, as she used to do whenever she asked me to dance and sing in front of my classmates. I reminded her of "Blood Sea," the women's emancipation song: how I would sing it in front of the class, while she sang with me from the back of the classroom with flushed cheeks.

On that day, she closed her tiny stand for several hours.

Like almost everyone, Teacher Oh had two jobs. In the morning, she taught students at a small school, where half of the students didn't come regularly. In the afternoon, she came to the market to sell bread. She didn't have time to bake it herself, so she bought it from old ladies who baked in their houses but couldn't compete with the loud voices of other vendors. She didn't make much money at the market, but it was better than just staying in the house and not even trying to escape her poverty.

Holding my hands, she smiled bitterly and said, "I had no idea that selling things to other people could be so hard. But what else can I do! I already sold all my beloved books."

She had been an ideal teacher. She was honest and didn't abuse her authority like other teachers. She had taught Kim Il Sung's books passionately, and we had studied together as friends would.

"You know, Jia, life can change in a flash, or lead you in an unexpected direction. Nothing is as precious as life.

Trust me, I have seen death with my own eyes…" Her eyes looked much older because of the deep wrinkles that ran from their edges.

She continued, "My husband and daughter died on the same day. How could I have imagined such a hell? My youngest daughter always clung to my skirt, complaining about how noisy her stomach was, and one day, after she came back from the school, she seemed to have no energy left. But, you know, people are all like that now, so I didn't care. I was sick of hearing her complain—it only made me hungrier. I was tired of telling her that our Dear Leader would soon solve all the problems. The longer the situation continued, the more restless I became. When I saw my neighbors heading to the markets and not to their usual jobs, I knew I should do something too. But I couldn't leave the country and become a capitalist merchant: my life, devoted to the Party and its ideology, would have lost all meaning. I ignored my husband's suggestion to start selling our goods. I mocked him and told him his brain was being rotted by hunger."

Just then, two *kkotjebi* ran past us, like bullets shot out of a gun. Behind them, a young woman, who looked much younger than me, shouted, "Damn you! I'll kill you next time I see you."

Teacher Oh stopped speaking. Her eyes followed the *kkotjebi,* who held new shoes in their hands and disappeared around a corner. She heaved a deep and long sigh.

"When my daughter came back from school, she was quiet and spoke in a low voice. 'Mom, I'm sleepy,' she said. 'I slept all day in class. I didn't know until the teacher woke me up that class already finished. On the way home, I walked half asleep. I almost sank down on the ground, and I'm still sleepy.' Then she fell asleep in a corner of the room, and died. My husband and I realized it only after several hours. He went crazy. He cried out, "How can be this possible? My daughter just died in front of me. What a bad father I am! We killed our own daughter." Then he fell down and died on the spot. In just one day, I had to send both my daughter and husband to the other world. I didn't cry. I didn't have time. I had to take care of two other kids. I decided not to be stuck in the house anymore. That's why I came here and why I'm shouting to sell one more piece of bread every day."

We looked at the other vendors, yelling at the top of their voices next to us.

"I would sell clothes or shoes like them if I were handy, but I can't make them." Teacher Oh sighed. "What's worse, I'm not smart like the other women here, who hang around the brokers. They get goods at low prices from those brokers."

While she spoke, she kept urging me to eat her bread.

"I'm not attractive anymore, I don't have a smooth tongue. I know how to handle kids, not adults."

When I was about to leave, she stuffed three pieces of bread in my pocket.

"But, I'm the luckiest and happiest woman in this place. My ex-students help me. Sometimes, they bring clothes from China and give them to me for very little. I never thought I would be obliged to my little students like this."

Saying good-bye, she gave me a wide smile. "Jia, my life hasn't been so bad! After you leave, I will smile and think about those days. How cute you were! What a terrible teacher I was!"

I bought most of her bread, claiming that I was about to buy lunch for my coworkers in the market. On that day, my coworkers had to fill their stomachs with Teacher Oh's bread.

7

Sun's Story

Sun was my neighbor. Her flat was right next to mine, in the rusty apartment complex I had been living in for the past few years. Sometime after moving in, I met her mother, Aunt Cho, in the hall. She asked about my age, my job—all the usual questions that arise when people meet each other for the first time.

"Why don't you live with your parents?"

I answered instantly: "They're dead. I've never seen them."

"Oh…" She nodded her head slowly, looking ill at ease, and let me pass by.

Whenever Aunt Cho stopped by my house after that, she would look around my kitchen and then disappear. Several minutes later, she would come back with dishes in her hands, and one of them always held *kimchi*.

"I worked in the Nutrition Department before I had Sun, so I know how to handle cooking. You can trust my food, and you should gain at least five kilograms."

I couldn't decline her kindness—her *kimchi* was the best I had ever eaten. With each bite of the pickled cabbage, I felt my stomach grow so clean and cool. I brought any cookies or snacks I could get in the hotel to her house, and though I insisted she try them, Aunt Cho always put them aside, saying, "Sun might like these more than me; she'll be back next week. I'm sure she'll like you a lot—she always wanted a sister."

Sun was 19 years old, with white skin and red lips. When I finally met her, I couldn't believe that she had just returned from three months of volunteering in the countryside before graduating from a teaching school; it seemed her skin had special protection against the sun. She was a giddy girl, and she followed me around, talking about everything she saw and heard. We liked to go to the street market to look at cosmetics. We couldn't afford to buy anything; we just went to be together and enjoy the uproarious atmosphere.

Sun's favorite topic was her boyfriend, Gun. She had met him while walking with her friends in the Kaesŏn Youth Park, on a Saturday. Sun said the day was brighter than usual, or maybe the significance of her first encounter with Gun made her memory of it brighter. She and her friends enjoyed walking there more than in any other park in Pyongyang because it was usually full of young people. A dark-skinned man with thick eyebrows had approached the group and smiled at Sun. She said she liked his bright and even teeth. Most young girls didn't like guys with swarthy skin, because it reminded them of laborers, but Sun said Gun was different. He had great, sharp eyes, and he worked in the dancing and singing propaganda unit of a big factory. When I saw him the first time, I couldn't help but understand why Sun praised him.

Sun was happy and dreamed of a future shared with her boyfriend. When she became a teacher in an elementary school, she loved talking about her students. She devoted all her energy to them and recorded each student's characteristics in a notebook.

"You know what? I heard such a funny thing from my students today," she said, sitting in my apartment one afternoon. "They said they like middle-aged female teachers the best. You know why? Because young single female teachers like me don't have to cook and take care of their own children and husbands. And we don't wash our clothes, because our mothers do it. In the morning we have only to do our makeup and eat the breakfast prepared by our mothers. So we have a lot of energy left when we come to school. But middle-aged female teachers have to do these chores every day for their families; their hands are never dry of water. When they beat the students, it doesn't hurt, because they don't have any energy left. But we have a lot of energy, so our palms are the harshest. You can't imagine how cute they were when they said that."

Sun's family was not untouched by the famine of 1995: her students started to skip school to go beg for food at the market. She and the other teachers searched the markets after class, trying to persuade their students to return to school. She came home every night bone tired. I loved her. I watched her tenderly, as my sister had watched over me.

In the summer of 1997, I didn't see Sun for several weeks. I missed her, but I decided not to begrudge her time with others. Then, one night, I heard her call my name, and when I opened my window, she was standing outside, like a ghost.

"What happened, Sun?"

"He's gone. He disappeared without saying anything to me."

She wore a thin shirt, though the night was cool, and her face was practically blue. I took her hand and led her into my room. I watched her as she cried quietly with her legs folded under her and her hands on her knees. I thought it must be the worst time in her life. I didn't say anything; I just let her cry.

At length, she told me that Gun and his family were gone in one night, and no one knew where. No!—everybody knew, but no one would say. The steps Gun's family took one day might be what other neighbors were driven to the next. Sun said that the shoe factory where Gun's parents worked had closed several months before, and Gun was trying to sell their household goods in the street market. Gun's older brother had died at age 21 in an accident while performing military duties, and his death had driven Gun's parents to despair. Since then, his parents' health had been Gun's priority.

Sun couldn't understand why Gun hadn't mentioned leaving. A couple of days earlier, he had asked for a picture of them together. She was devastated that he hadn't shared his plans with her.

I didn't see Sun much after that night. I couldn't offer consolation, and I couldn't blame Gun: such was our situation and our lives. Time for despair could be better used looking for a way to survive. All I hoped for Sun was that she would forget about Gun as soon as possible. As time went by, Sun would learn what I already knew too well: the more you miss people who have already left you, the more pain you feel.

Several weeks later, I ran into Sun in the hall of the building, and she smiled at me. I asked her to come by my apartment whenever she had some free time. She didn't seem to have changed too much—she was still cheerful—but as we chatted she sometimes lost her train of thought and grew silent. I thought time would solve her problems.

Late one night, she came over, and I noticed that she had become emaciated.

"Can I stay with you tonight?" Sun asked with a low voice. Her eyes were unusually shiny.

I pulled her into my room with delight; I had been afraid she was avoiding me, and it was wonderful to have her in my apartment again. We didn't sleep much—I just held her hand under the blanket while we talked, as my sister used to. Sun talked a lot, laughing unnaturally hard, and told me about how she and Gun had dreamed of their future together, with a house and children.

Suddenly, her eyes filled with fear. "I'm afraid, sister. Nothing seems sure in this world. I still don't understand why Gun didn't discuss anything with me. Before he left, he even talked about our wedding. We were going to take pictures on Mansu Hill—we thought the gold of Kim Il Sung's statue in the background would make the pictures more colorful. But he left the next day. Do you think he left because he didn't want to marry me? Did I pressure him too much? I really didn't care about the wedding; that wasn't important. He misunderstood me."

I smoothed her hair. "Sometimes people can't be together forever, even though they would like to be. Don't blame him too much. There must be some reason he had to leave that way."

We cried together. I cried for my grandparents and my sister. Since the night before Seunggyu had left for the countryside, I couldn't get them off my mind. In my dream, I saw their bodies drifting on filthy floodwater. Seunggyu and his soldiers pushed them away, cursing them with cold eyes.

Sun cried for Gun. She couldn't stop blaming him, but she prayed for his safety. I consoled myself with the thought that everyone in this world had their own sadness to contend with, and ours might not be the worst.

The next day, Sun was gone. Her mother said Sun had left to see relatives, and I didn't ask her anything more, though I could hear sobbing through the walls. To her parents, Sun was a treasure. They had her when they were both over 40, after they had given up on ever having a child. They had waited for her for 20 years and lost her in just one day.

The previous night, in my room, Sun had smiled at me and laughed more than usual. I knew that she had decided to look for Gun in China, and I also knew there was nothing I could do to stop her; I couldn't even tell her I knew of her plans. I felt deeply sad. Gradually, I was losing every familiar face around me.

I never expected to hear from her again.

8

Gun's Story

Several months passed, and the signs of famine persisted in the city. Winter made people even more desperate. We were adjusting to the possibility that family members, relatives, neighbors—people with whom we had exchanged smiles hours before—might disappear without a trace.

In factories and offices, lunch was no longer provided. Whether we worked or not hardly mattered, as showing up for a job often didn't result in food or wages. Kim Jong Il's regime emphasized that we could overcome this hardship by working together, but words do not fill an empty stomach, and the search for food drove people to desperate measures.

One winter evening, I went to bed early, and was staring at the ceiling through the darkness. The government shut off power to residences at 8:30 P.M., and the city plunged into impenetrable darkness. In those days of darkness, and with Sun gone, I was spending more nights at the hotel than at home, out of loneliness. The hotel was empty, but the manager was ordered to keep lights on in 20 rooms to make the city look a little alive. That night, however, I thought I should return home; I felt guilty, having left my room empty for several days. My apartment was not any bigger than Aunt Ann's, but somehow being alone made me feel the cold more keenly, so I tried to fall asleep as quickly as possible. Just as I was drifting off, I heard a cautious knock at my door. At first I thought it was a rat, struggling to find food, but the sound became louder and more insistent. Eventually, I got up and put an ear to the door.

"Jia! Jia!" a low voice came through.

"Who is it?" I was afraid. Nobody had come by my home in the wee hours since Sun had gone. "Who is it?" I rasped again.

"Jia, it's me. It's Gun."

I tripped over myself struggling to pull some clothes on.

"Jia. Please let me in."

I opened the door a crack, but the light was off, and I couldn't see anything. It hadn't worked for many days. After the electricity shortage, the government had supplied power from 5:00 to 8:00 A.M. and from 6:00 to 11:00 P.M., but even that soon became irregular. They would only supply electricity to apartments whose residents gave them extra money. My building didn't want to pay extra money; people relied on kerosene lamps.

Before my eyes adjusted to the darkness, I was as good as blind.

"It's Gun. Don't you remember my voice?"

I could hear the desperation in his voice, and opened the door at once; a black figure rushed into the room. When my eyes finally adjusted, I recognized him.

"Heavens! What are you doing here? Didn't you leave?" I seated him on the sofa, but he dropped to the floor, heaving a sigh of relief as he saw my fear dissolve.

"I came back for Sun, but there was no way to contact her except through you. I waited for her half the day, hiding on the other side of the building, but I didn't see her. Could you bring her here?"

He smiled. I could see teeth were still white and even. I could read the happiness in his eyes and his haste to see her. I watched him for a while, and his smile slowly died as we spoke.

"Could you? Is it too difficult? Maybe it's not the right time to call her..." Gun scratched the top of his head over and over again.

I spoke slowly. "She is not here anymore, Gun."

His smile disappeared altogether, and he sat upright in front of me. "What do you mean? Why isn't she here anymore? Did she leave for someplace else?"

I held his hand and said gently, "Gun, she left after you did. I'm sure she left a note with her parents. I haven't seen it, so I don't know exactly where she is right now. But I think she left to look for you."

His mouth hung open, and his stare was blank. Silence lingered between us for a time.

"How could this happen? It's my fault. It's my fault... I should have come back faster."

Gun sobbed in front of me. I let him cry as much as he wanted, just as I had with Sun.

"If I had come back a little faster... If I had left her a

note before I ran…this would never have happened."

Gun told me that he had hesitated before running away. He hadn't wanted to leave without Sun, but there was no choice. He had heard that in China and other countries people could eat as much as they wanted. The government told us the floods had hit the entire world and that people in other countries were suffering more than we were. But while running an errand for his factory, Gun had traveled to Sinŭiju, a ghost town on the Chinese border, and had witnessed the land of China beyond the Amrok River. He was stunned. He couldn't take his eyes off it—the high buildings and splendid lights were in such sharp contrast to the dark and barren Sinŭiju. Gun imagined plentiful food for his parents there—how would the Chinese have money for all that light unless they were well fed? The loving son couldn't stand letting his parents grow sicker from starvation.

Gun had crossed the border with his elderly parents—a dangerous journey. They settled in a small Korean-Chinese village, where Gun worked day and night, but he could not forget Sun. His parents knew that returning to North Korea was much more dangerous than getting out, but they couldn't stop him. They couldn't bear to see their son's face so empty any longer.

Gun had returned here to take Sun with him to China.

Gun knew that China wasn't very safe, especially for a woman, and that it wasn't the happy land they had imagined. He knew now that he'd have to return to China to find Sun, as quickly as possible. He could only hope that no ill fortune had befallen her.

He lifted his head and turned his reddened eyes to me.

"You really don't have any idea where she is? Didn't she leave a note? Not even to you?"

"I'm sorry, Gun. Nobody knows where she is, or how she is. She slept here the night before she left. I guessed she would try to track you down, but I didn't stop her. No one could have. You must understand, you know how determined she is."

He sighed deeply. "It's my fault. It's all my fault. I needed money to come back here. I worked in factories, farms—anywhere I could make money. But I didn't return in time."

"Gun. You must go back to China and find her. She's a smart girl. I'm sure she's safe and she's looking for you."

He shook his head. "Jia, you don't know about that place. How can I find her? We are inferior to insects over there. Here we have no hope, but at least we're regarded as human. Over there, we're just trash. No one even looks at us." Gun grabbed his head again. It was too much to think of Sun, alone in China.

He suddenly stood up in the darkness. "I have to go, Jia. I should go back now and find her. The sooner, the better."

With that, Gun disappeared as suddenly as he had come. I didn't have time to ask about his parents' health, or his life on the other side. The execution of runaways was increasing, but that didn't stop people from trying to cross the river. The hunger wracking their bodies every moment of every day gave them no choice. All I could do was pray for Gun and Sun, and for the others who had gone the same route.

I understood the fear and the hope that filled those who chose to run. Sun probably left with the fear of stepping into a strange land, but warmed with the excitement of finding her love again. Gun's love for his parents and for

Sun, and Sun's love for him, were good reasons to undertake the dangerous journey. I had no one. In a way, having no family insulated me from the famine. I had Seunggyu, but he couldn't see the shadows of my past and therefore never really knew me.

I was breathing every moment, but I wasn't alive.

Before returning to the border to cross back into China, Gun had to deliver medicine to his uncle here. His father was always worried about his brother's chronic stomach disease and had packed some supplies in Gun's bag. The house wasn't far from Sun's, and in darkness Gun felt safer as he moved through the streets.

He sneaked into the village where his uncle lived, knowing the layout very well, as he had spent so much time there playing with his cousin, Jaeho, when he was young. The village was also completely dark, and when he knocked on the door of his uncle's house, everyone seemed to be asleep.

At the door, Gun quietly called out his cousin's name. "Jaeho, Jaeho, are you there?"

A tense voice came through the door. "Who's there?" It was his uncle.

Gun breathed again. "It's me. It's Gun."

There was silence inside for a moment, and then the door opened a tiny crack. Gun couldn't see anything, and his uncle seemed to hesitate for the same reason.

"It's me, Uncle. It's Gun. I've come back."

His uncle opened the door and stepped outside. He touched Gun's cheek. "Where have you been? I've had no news about your family. Let's go inside." He grabbed Gun's hand and led him into the house.

His uncle's wife, Jiyoung, and their son, Jaeho, had awakened and were looking at him in surprise.

"We've been outside the country," Gun said. "Did our sudden disappearance cause you any trouble?" He nodded to his aunt and Jaeho.

"It has been all right. Some investigators stopped by the house several times to inquire about your family, but as you know, we knew nothing. We were so surprised when we heard the news."

Gun felt sorry for his uncle; he knew his father and uncle had depended on each other after losing their parents at a young age.

Jaeho was blunt: "Why did you come back? You're endangering our family." As only children, Gun and Jaeho had been like brothers, and yet now Jaeho avoided Gun's eyes. Jaeho must have felt abandoned, just as Sun had.

"I just want to give this medicine to Uncle, then I'll leave." Gun turned to his uncle. "How's your stomach? Is it any better?"

Gun reached into his bag and produced the medicine and some money. His uncle looked at the offerings in surprise, but his wife snatched the money without delay.

Scowling at his wife, Gun's uncle said to Gun, "It's only an old people's disease. I don't need medicine, don't bring it next time."

"Father wanted me to bring it; he's always worrying about you. You can't imagine how sad he is to be away from you right now."

His uncle started sobbing and murmured, "He doesn't know how my heart broke after he left without a word. My life has come to a dead end. I wonder if I will see his face again before I die."

Gun held his hand. "Don't be sad, Uncle. I'm sure you'll meet soon." Gun was overcome with guilt at having divided his family.

Jaeho grumbled something and lay down, drawing the blanket over his head.

Gun stood up. "I'll leave now. It will be much safer for your family and for me."

"No, stay here, just for one day, Gun," the old man said, tugging at Gun's shirt. "You can leave tomorrow. I want to hear the news about my brother."

To Gun, darkness was preferable for a safe escape, and he wanted to search for Sun as soon as possible, but his uncle turned to him with tear-filled eyes. Gun looked at his aunt and his cousin, but they were silent; Jaeho lay motionless under the blanket.

"It will be all right. Nobody visits our house," Gun's uncle said. "Bring your shoes inside. You should eat something—aren't you hungry?"

Gun couldn't turn down his uncle's offer; he didn't know if he would ever see him again. "Okay, I'll leave tomorrow night," he said, setting down his bag and pushing it to the corner. Then he told them the story of how he had crossed the river with his father and mother.

Jaeho whined, "I have to get up early tomorrow. I can't sleep with all this talk."

Gun lay down next to his uncle and talked all night long in a low voice about his family's life in China. His uncle tried not to miss a single word. Whenever Gun mentioned his father, his uncle sobbed. Gun decided not to tell him about his father's foot, which had been almost useless since he had stepped on a piece of glass while crossing the river. Though they were able to extract the piece of glass and disinfect his foot, the wound wouldn't heal, and it continued to cause his father pain. They couldn't find any medicine and were too afraid to ask for help.

Gun and his uncle fell asleep at dawn and didn't hear Jaeho leave. Gun slept a long and deep sleep.

He woke to someone shaking his body violently.

Gun saw that he was surrounded by soldiers. Something was wrong. He tried to stand up right away, but they kicked at his ribs, and he rolled over in pain.

"Get up, national traitor! You are not worthy of sleeping in this house. Get your butt off the floor." Two soldiers held Gun's arms and pulled him along by force. He was led out of his uncle's house as they kicked him in the abdomen, the calves, his head. How did they know? Had he slept too long? Had someone seen him sneak into the house?

A square-faced soldier ordered the others to stop kicking him, and a truncheon came down on him, hitting him hard in the right thigh.

"Get up! Don't exaggerate the pain." The square-faced soldier swatted at Gun with the truncheon.

Gun could barely raise himself. He had witnessed this scene so often in his dreams. Didn't someone say dreams implied the opposite of what would really happen?

He stood up, shaking, and his uncle and aunt came into sight. His uncle's tear-filled eyes were fearful, but his aunt avoided Gun's face. One soldier pulled his hand behind him and another fastened handcuffs on his wrists.

"He hasn't eaten anything yet today," his uncle said, approaching the square-faced soldier and appealing to him.

The soldier scowled. "What did you say? Did you say you want to feed that national traitor?"

Gun's uncle shrank back in fear.

"Did you receive something from him?" the soldier demanded.

"No, nothing..." Gun's aunt answered.

"If we find something in your house, your family will be punished like him. Understood?" The soldier stared at them, brandishing the truncheon liberally. "Where is your son? According to him, your family isn't related to this reactionary element's family."

Gun didn't understand this. What did this mean? No, he decided not to understand what the soldier was saying, what this meant. The soldier turned back to Gun and smiled, watching him in silence. Then he held the truncheon to Gun's face and whispered in his ear, "Welcome back to North Korea." He pointed at the other soldiers with his truncheon. "Take him to the car," he ordered.

The soldiers rushed toward him and dragged him into the back of an army car. They got in and sat around him.

Gun could hear his uncle protesting. "General, he must have been influenced by some reactionary elements—he has never disobeyed the rules, he was a model for his factory!"

The square-faced soldier addressed his men, ignoring the pleas of Gun's uncle. "Search the whole house. If you find something, report it to me later. We must go."

"Gun! Gun!" his uncle shouted. Gun didn't look back. His uncle cried, "This is my fault. I shouldn't have asked you to stay here overnight. How can I face my brother in the other world? This is my fault!"

As the car pulled away, Gun realized he had forgotten to tell to his uncle about the medicine. He had to take the medicine twice a day, not three times, like medicine in North Korea. Chinese medicine was much stronger.

9

To Become a Spy

Gun was thrown into a cell already overflowing with prisoners. He looked around the cell and realized he had been dragged into an underground prison. He had heard about these places, deep in the mountains: he had heard that people sent to them never returned. Runaways to China lived in fear of being caught by the Chinese police, handed over to the North Korean police, and sent to one of these prisons.

Most prisoners crouched and bowed their heads, just looking at the ground. The smell of urine filled the air, and nausea overcame Gun as he approached a woman whose chin was resting on her chest. She was slumped on the floor, and looked more like a corpse than a human being, her enormous belly dwarfing her tiny head. "That bitch pees more than five times a day on that spot. She can't even wait until toilet time. I can't stand it anymore," one man complained, looking at Gun.

"What's wrong with her?" Gun asked. No wonder there was space around her. An old woman stared at the grumbling man and said, "Don't talk like that. Pregnant women have to go to the restroom more frequently because of the baby's pressure."

"Who wants a baby now!" the man sneered. "Besides, her baby's butt has two different cheeks: one from China and the other from here. It must be deformed." Some of the men around him smirked.

A policeman kicked at the iron bars. "Cut it out, national traitors! Do you fucking bastards want me to stop your laughing?"

The pregnant woman didn't seem to care how people talked about her; she didn't raise her head or move at all. Gun couldn't help but sit next to her, as finding another place to lie down in the cell was impossible.

He wondered what Sun was doing at that moment. She must blame me, he thought. Why didn't I leave as soon as I delivered the medicine to my uncle? What about Jaeho? Was he afraid the police would raid his house and arrest everyone for harboring a traitor? If Jaeho hadn't said anything, nobody would have known; Gun could have said farewell to his uncle and his family, safely crossed the river, and started looking for Sun. Jaeho's betrayal seemed coldhearted; if it was revenge for Gun's leaving without telling him, it was too cruel.

A policeman opened the door of the prison cell abruptly. "Hey, new guy! Come out." When Gun looked up toward the voice, three men were standing behind the policeman. Together they dragged Gun to another room, similar in size to the cell, though its emptiness made it feel much bigger and colder. A yellowish, umbrella-shaped light hung from the middle of the ceiling—the only decoration. Directly under it, in a chair, sat the square-faced soldier who had arrested him, with his legs crossed, smoking. Gun felt a chill that sank to the marrow of his bones; whether from the cold or from the man's vicious smile, he didn't know. He decided instantly that the fastest way out was to acquiesce. He stood at attention before his interrogator.

"We investigated you and your family's history thoroughly. Up to now you've had no problems with the government, and yet you chose to destroy everything. How was China? Was crossing the border worth betraying your country?" Gun's interrogator waved his cigarette back and forth.

Gun said nothing; there was nothing to say. He wondered how many times a day that man examined runaways, and how much information they must beat out of each one. It frightened him. The square-faced man seemed uninterested in any answers Gun might provide; he just kept smoking. Gun didn't raise his eyes.

Back in the cell, Gun was lying on the floor when he felt warm water spread underneath him. It felt so good; he wanted to take off his clothes and soak his whole body in it. When he opened his eyes, he realized that it had come from between the pregnant woman's legs. He met her eyes and she smiled, though her face was filled with shame. "Sorry," she said in a low voice, but Gun didn't complain. In fact, he didn't care. The smell of urine didn't bother him anymore.

Gun was dragged back to the room again the next day and beaten by the same men, the same way. They weren't even trying to extract information from him, and after a while he didn't feel pain anymore; his body had swelled to almost three times its normal size. All he heard, all day, was "national traitor." When Gun was returned to the cell after a day of beatings, other prisoners consoled him, saying, "It's just the first step. We all passed it, and it'll be over soon. Just hang on a little longer."

What had he done? Gun had been a good citizen in North Korea: never disobeyed the law, never went against the order of the government—in fact, he was the most enthusiastic member of the Propaganda Department in the factory where he worked. He hadn't crossed the border to betray his country; he just wanted to make a living and not starve to death. More important than that, he didn't want his parents to starve to death. He had waited for the government to help them, he had believed the government would do something, but nothing had happened. The situation only got worse, until crossing the river was the only way.

The pregnant woman fed Gun the rice-and-corn soup they were given, because he was bound and couldn't hold a spoon himself. The soup was thin, but it helped restore energy to his injured body.

"How old are you?" he asked one day, as she put a spoonful to his mouth.

Her face turned red and she responded, hesitantly, "Seventeen."

"How did you become pregnant at such a young age?" Gun asked the question despite himself.

She fed him another spoonful, looking into his face. "When I got over to China with my father the first time, he sold me to a Chinese man. But it was for me—he did it for me." She put the spoon in the bowl and went on,

"I was actually happy over there. People blame my father, but I don't care; my Chinese husband was really nice. We couldn't communicate very well—sometimes we needed his Korean-Chinese friend or neighbor—but the language barrier didn't cause too much trouble." She spoke softly, so others couldn't hear.

"He was fifteen years older than me, and very poor. To buy me, he spent almost all of the money he had saved, but I never missed a meal; he always tried to feed me well. When I got pregnant, we didn't know what to do. We were so happy, but we were afraid because we knew we shouldn't have children. His friends had warned us that a pregnancy would risk my safety, but we weren't cautious enough. If the Chinese government found out I was from North Korea, I would be dragged back here. We knew we had to give up the baby, and walking to the hospital, we cried bitterly in the street, holding hands. Some policemen happened to pass us—two blubbering adults holding hands, who wouldn't notice? We were so ignorant. They asked what had happened. I panicked and started to run, but they caught me. When they found out who I was, they sent me here. My husband tried to have me released, but the poor man has no power."

She caressed her belly. "I saved my baby, but I lost my husband."

Gun looked at her belly. He wanted to ask her whether she had seen Sun in her village. Sun could easily be in a similar situation, but he couldn't bear to imagine it. He bit his lower lip hard. No! Asking such questions would only bring bad fortune.

Gun was plagued by nightmares. In one he saw Sun, her naked body in chains, suspended from a big brick wall. She struggled to cut the chains, but if she cut one, another came out of the brick and bound her more tightly. She was crying out and bleeding, but as she wriggled, the chains pulled her into the wall. She called for Gun over and over; it felt so real. He could feel his breath quicken, watching her desperately, unable to reach her as she was gradually sucked into the brick. In the end, her whole body was engulfed; the brick wall turned so peaceful and shiny, with no scars on its brown face.

Sometimes, the dreams were happier. Sun would smile, wearing her bright, pretty *hanbok,* as she walked arm in arm with a man in Chinese clothes. They looked so intimate and were always walking away. Whenever he had those dreams, Gun woke up in a cold sweat. He didn't like either one.

On the eighth day of Gun's incarceration, he was given two meals of corn, along with salty water and cabbage, and sent to another prison cell. There, he found four men seated, one in each corner. They all seemed to be around his age, but they looked like half-wits. They were eerily quiet; he could hardly hear them breathe. Gun wandered around the room for a while and finally sat in the center of the room. No one spoke. Since they all had the same stories of torture to tell, there was no point in sharing them.

It was a new setting, but the investigators asked the same questions, and Gun gave the same answers. They beat him for yet another week. He had to kneel down on the ground, and his hands were tied behind his back so that he couldn't move. That was the daily routine. Beginning early in the morning, they kicked his face and his body, and sent him back to the cell at night. They gave him a spoon without a handle, so he wouldn't commit suicide or make a weapon. He was never allowed to wash, and soon enough he was giving off the same smell as the prisoners he first met. He wondered about the pregnant girl, but there was no way to find out what happened to her.

Then things changed: they began interrogating him and torturing him at the same time. The square-faced man showed up again.

"How have you been? You look much fatter than before. I didn't know you were so satisfied with this place."

He sat down on a worn-out wooden chair so wide that he needed only the right half, and set his cigarette down on the left. "So, where are your parents?"

Gun's stomach spouted a lump of acid. "They're dead. Please, believe me: that's why I came back here—I was lonely and missed my relatives. I won't run away anymore, and I really regret doing it the first time. Please, please forgive me." Gun thought the square-faced man was his last hope.

The square-faced man was not moved by Gun's confession. He simply lit another cigarette and asked his subordinates, "Where is the kettle?"

A big, round kettle was brought in. The man asked again, "Are you sure your parents are dead?"

"How could old people survive such a fast current?" Gun cried. "We were stupid, we tried to cross the river, but it was the worst decision of my life. I regret it to the bone."

The square-faced man stroked his stubbly chin. The back of his hand was flecked with tiny scars and scabs. Grinning lightly, he trilled, "Start."

Two men made Gun lie down and forced his mouth open. Holding his lower jaw down, they poured water into his mouth from the yellowish metal kettle, and though he tried not to swallow it, the pressure of the water made it rush fiercely down his throat. When his stomach was full, they stamped on his torso until water came out of his mouth and anus—every orifice in his body—and he vomited white liquid. Gun felt his eyes would shoot out; his legs kicked in every direction, and his wrists wriggled in the grip of the men holding him down. They repeated this procedure several times.

The square-faced man finally came and crouched down next to Gun, watching him from above, so that his face appeared to be upside down. "So, did I see ghosts in China? I had dinner with your parents four days ago. Your mother cooked bean paste stew for me. Bean paste stew, with green onions and tofu. Isn't that her best dish? I don't understand why you left such nice parents so readily—they looked so sad not to be able to see you, but I said you were fine with me. They were so happy and relieved to hear those words!"

Gun realized why they had stopped asking about his parents. He grabbed the square-faced man's arm. He couldn't help stuttering, "Please—spare their lives. They are too old to handle this. They just followed me. I planned everything by myself."

The man grinned. "I can treat them as my real parents," he sneered. "I'm sure they'll take to me, but what can you do for me? Taking care of old people, as you know, isn't easy, especially in the case of your limping father…"

Gun kept his grip on the man's arm, white liquid still running from his mouth. They looked at each other for a while, and Gun felt he would never forget that steel block of a face. Then the man stood up, took his cigarette from the chair, and said, "Send him back to his cell."

As he was dragged from the room, Gun felt capable of murder for the first time in his life.

For a week after that, Gun was left alone. As soon as his body recovered, however, the beatings resumed, lasting for ten more days. Whenever he asked about his parents, the blows came even harder, and Gun begged over and over to be taken to the square-faced man. He shuddered with fear at the thought of his parents coming to harm, but no solution presented itself. Gun was sure they wanted something from him, or he would have been executed immediately.

Gun's body was no longer his own. Even his voice sounded foreign when they demanded he sing the revolutionary hymns he learned in kindergarten and recite the Great Leader's instructions. After several weeks, he was on the brink of total collapse. And then the harassment stopped.

The policemen took him and the four other men into the shower room and they were given their first shower in months. Then, a regular meal—meat soup and rice. Gun couldn't swallow the food at first and was wary of being poisoned, but they threatened him and the others until they cleaned their plates. Their stomachs didn't trust the food—all five rushed to the toilets after finishing. Within a few days, they were able to digest solid food, and the torturers even brought roasted chicken and sausages. The smell was irresistible, though every time Gun was offered a meal, he felt it could be his last. This treatment lasted for two weeks.

Once their bodies had grown stronger, the prisoners were called to a large, clean office they hadn't seen before. They were treated differently, almost like humans.

The square-faced man wore a dark-green army uniform and sat behind a desk, resting his feet on the gray desktop. "Come in, my comrades, make yourselves comfortable," he bellowed, dusting off his round army hat, which looked much older than his tidy uniform. He blew on the hat roughly and pulled it onto his head; it emphasized the squareness of his face. He locked his fingers together, rested his forearms on the edge of his desk, and stretched his neck out toward them.

They tried to figure out how they had progressed from being national traitors to being comrades.

"There is good news. You should appreciate the kindness of the government. You were supposed to pay the penalty for the crime you committed, but the government has decided to forgive you—only you five. You're chosen people; you might have been prisoners forever, finishing your lives in that filthy jail, but the government has shown mercy. We'll let you slip, under certain conditions, which means we will give you a mission to strengthen the government."

Gun was at a loss, and the others seemed unconvinced.

"You'll be special agents, assigned to catch national traitors in China. From now on, you will be heroes for North Korea—not traitors anymore, but heroes—for your country and your families."

With a satisfied smile, he slowly looked from one man's face to the next.

Part 3

10

False Identity

The winter of 1997 was unusually long, and Pyongyang met the New Year without celebration. It seemed no one was interested in welcoming 1998.

Even the *Magnolia kobus* blossoms on Okryu street seemed reluctant to show their faces. On a clear January morning, Seunggyu and I were walking north from the Taedong Bridge and ended up at the Taedong Resort, where we stopped to look at the biggest bridge in Pyongyang, Okryu Bridge. From there I could clearly see the Great Leader's calligraphy, "Ok-Ryu-Gyo," on the bridge's parapet.

Every morning, Okryu Bridge filled with people rushing from their houses to downtown Pyongyang. The bridge was the gift of the Great Leader, Kim Il Sung, to the people in 1960, to ease their commute. Before that time, they had to use the crowded Taedong Bridge or take a boat. Thanks to the Great Leader, the largest bridge in the city was built.

Strangely, from our vantage point, I couldn't see anyone on the bridge.

I kept looking, though, as I was trying to avoid Seung-gyu's eyes. I didn't want him to see my swollen eyelids; Aunt Ann had left the hotel the previous day, and I had spent the night crying.

Several of the cooks and I had thrown a small farewell party for her, and Cook Kim had even sneaked two plates of rice cakes. I brought a pack of the Korean traditional snack that I had stashed in my room, and Cook Kim set out too many cups of water, so the table wouldn't feel so empty.

"That's the best way to taste the real taste of rice cakes—with a draft of water in your mouth," he said, convincing no one. "First, drink some water: it moistens the inside of your mouth. Then chew one bite of the rice cake, then, drink more water. You can feel the cake melting in your mouth."

Each of us took one cup with a smile, but there were still at least five cups left.

"You had better take two cups; today's rice cakes are pretty sticky," he said, laughing, handing out another cup to each of us. On any other day, Aunt Ann would have teased Cook Kim, but she was in no mood that day. The hotel managers had recommended that Aunt Ann stop working because of her age.

"You know I don't have any problems using my body. I always have worked harder than those useless guards, and I don't get tired. I have never slacked off," Aunt Ann said, with a sulky face. She was still in her uniform.

She was always brisk, and I never heard her complain about being overworked. Of all the workers, she should have left the hotel last, not first.

"Have you decided where to go?" I asked her.

Aunt Ann turned to me. "The hotel manager said I can have my old house back in my hometown, Wŏnsan. He already contacted the town governor so I wouldn't have a problem, but I can't live there again." She fidgeted with the cup, setting it on the table in front of her. It was cruel for Aunt Ann to live by herself in the old house where she had lived with her family.

We were silent. Cook Kim handed her a soft, round cake smothered in black sesame seeds. "Take the house back anyway," he said. "Take everything the superiors promised you."

Aunt Ann was chewing her rice cake slowly; sesame seeds lined her upper lip. "I'm thinking about living with my second sister. She has just one son, and her house isn't so far from mine. I'll take the house, but I won't sleep there. I'll stay with my sister."

"What if the local officials discover you are staying somewhere else?" I asked, frowning at her with worry. "Moving around without permission of the government could cause trouble."

"Who cares?" Aunt Ann erupted. "There are empty houses everywhere, and it's impossible to check on the whereabouts of every person. Anyway, they're not going to care about an old woman like me."

I sang a song for her; she loved *Arirang* the best. Every night, when I stayed with her, I studied the *Arirang* songs of each province.

> Arirang, Arirang, Arari O!
> Crossing the hills of Arirang.
> There are twelve hills of Arirang
> And now I am crossing the last hill.

Many stars in the deep sky—
Many crimes in the life of man.
Arirang, Arirang, Arari O!
Crossing the hills of Arirang.

Arirang is the mountain of sorrow
And the path to Arirang has no returning.
Arirang, Arirang, Arari O!
Crossing the hills of Arirang.

Oh, twenty million countrymen
Where are you now?
Alive are only three thousand li of mountain
    and rivers.
Arirang, Arirang, Arari O!
Crossing the hills of Arirang.

Now I am an exile crossing the Amrok River
And the mountains and rivers of three
    thousand li are also lost.
Arirang, Arirang, Arari O!
Crossing the hills of Arirang.

I stayed with Aunt Ann for one last night. Ever since Gun's abrupt appearance and disappearance, I went home every night—I was afraid of missing Gun and Sun should they return and need my help.

I looked around the room at the hotel where Aunt Ann and I had lived as roommates for four years. It was too small for two people, but Aunt Ann was never angry with me and my messes. Even after twelve years, all of Aunt Ann's belongings fit in two small bags.

On that night, as with so many before it, we lay down and chatted until we fell asleep.

"I always wanted to have a daughter, so when I saw you for the first time, you don't know how happy it made me that we would live together," she said. "I felt, in place of my husband and son whom heaven took from me, I had been sent such a pretty daughter." Aunt Ann passed her hand over my hair. She sometimes cried while she slept, and I would pat her chest as though I was soothing a baby back to sleep. I wondered if she would do the same for me.

Thinking of her impending absence, my heart ached. I asked myself whether I had more luck in my life than other people. I had always been surrounded by good people, but sometimes I felt it wasn't luck, but rather a curse that I had to suffer. Whenever I made a friend, I had to prepare for the day when we would separate. I would never get used to it.

I wanted to be alone, but Seunggyu had insisted on dragging me down to Okryu Bridge. He couldn't understand why a janitor leaving was such a big deal to me. I had decided not to tell him about Sun and Gun; I didn't want to hear him curse my friends. Being outdoors didn't improve my mood, either. I didn't want to see the gaunt trees and the sleeping streets.

"So many people are leaving or disappearing," I said with a sigh, feeling empty—even of sadness.

"Don't talk like that, Jia," Seunggyu erupted. "Only losers run away; national traitors don't belong here anyway."

He took a round metal box out of the pocket of his gray pants. It was covered with yellow flowers and curved letters, and filled with fragrant sour and sweet candies.

"They're lemon flavored," Seunggyu said mildly, as though speaking to a child.

I didn't lift my eyes. "But Seunggyu, have you ever thought about why they are leaving, knowing that if they're caught, they'll be brutally punished?"

"Who cares what people think, Jia, it's a waste of time." Seunggyu threw a piece of candy into his mouth and blinked hard, several times. "Whoa! This was my favorite candy when I was a kid, but maybe not anymore…"

He could be incredibly stone-hearted, but I knew Seunggyu wasn't a cold person. He just didn't know how to express himself. I thought I could help him understand people who worked hard but could not be recognized because of their class.

"Why do you despise people who are different from you?" I asked. "No matter what class they belong to, they are also loyal to the Great Leader and to our country, but they're hungry. They have no control over their background; the only difference between you and them is that they were born into the wrong class, and that wasn't their choice."

He put a candy between my lips, to stop my mouth. Seeing my frown, he grinned and said, "Jia, they have bad blood and a reactionary tendency, you just don't see it. Our country is having a hard time right now, but we have to unite—that's the best and fastest way to recapture the way it was. Look at us! We're trying to overcome the hardship, we're loyal to the party and trust our leader. But these traitors screw everything up, thinking only about themselves. So selfish. They take public goods and run away at night like rats. They can't stand a little hunger."

Seunggyu put a candy in his mouth and pushed another toward mine, but I turned my head to avoid it.

"The second one is much better, Jia. If you give up because the first one was sour, you'll never get the real taste. Just endure the hard time for a short while. Don't avoid it. Runaways only look out for themselves. They don't want to put up with a little hardship for even one moment. What else could I call them but losers?"

Patting my shoulder, Seunggyu handed me the box. "Come on, Jia. I know you're upset about Aunt Ann, but you can't dwell on it. Let's think about ourselves and our future! I know today isn't the best day to look ahead, but the winter will be over soon, and I don't think spring will be long this year. Summer will come sooner or later. We need time to get through the trifling tasks of arranging a wedding."

He said his parents wanted to meet me and any of my living relatives. "My father is sure he must have known your parents or grandparents. He feels sorry he can't meet them. He has a broad set of acquaintances, you know." At this, Seunggyu gave me a big, confident smile.

That day, it became clear that it was time to tell Seunggyu my story. I couldn't hide anymore; I didn't want to. Seunggyu and I had been together for more than three years; I knew he had strong feelings for me, and I returned them. He loathed people with backgrounds like mine, but my background was part of me. No secret can stay buried forever. I hoped that hearing my story would overcome his prejudice against "those people."

The sooner I talked, the better.

The hotel grew busier. We had to divide up Aunt Ann's duties. There were no new recruits; when one person disappeared, we all picked up the slack. A week after Aunt Ann left, I called Seunggyu.

It was still too cold to be outside for long, but I felt it was the safest place to tell the story I had never told anyone. We sat side by side on a bench in Taedong Resort, as we had the week before, and I rested my right hand on his left. His hands were my favorite part of him—big enough to cover mine, which were chronically cold. I wasn't as nervous as I thought I would be, and once I began, telling the most important person in my life about my past felt like the most natural thing in the world. It felt good to share myself and be close to Seunggyu. Why hadn't I done it sooner?

Seunggyu was silent as I spoke. I didn't look at him, but I could feel him watching my face closely.

When I finished, he quietly stood up and said, "Let's go back. I'll take you home." His face was blushing deeply, like a scarlet peony.

It was the first time I had to reach for his hand, not he for mine. I could only hold three fingers; it was hard to grab his whole hand. As Seunggyu walked, he stared straight ahead, his mouth firmly closed. I knew it would be difficult for him to digest a woman's 20-year life story in a few hours—especially his future wife's hidden story—and I had tried to prepare for every reaction.

When we reached my apartment, Seunggyu peered up at the window on the third floor and said, "I have a two-week assignment training new recruits. I might not see you during that time."

His voice was distant. After that, he turned to go.

I called to him, "Seunggyu, can you understand now why I have sympathy for the people you despise?"

He nodded his head shortly, without looking back.

I decided not to be impetuous. No matter when it might be, the next time I saw Seunggyu I would tell him how mischievous I had been when I lived on the mountain. I climbed up to my flat and fell into a deep sleep.

Two days later, I arrived at the hotel in the morning and saw a man who looked like Seunggyu hastening down the hall past the front desk.

I caught up with him and touched his shoulder. "Seunggyu?"

He turned, and his panicked face stopped me in my tracks.

"What are you doing here?" I said. "Don't you have training for two whole weeks?"

The edges of his ears turned bright red, and he looked restlessly around the hall, apparently annoyed. "Right," he muttered. "I must go right now. I just had something to do for Jongmu here. I was just stopping by. I must go right now so I'm not late. See you in a couple weeks. I'll come by."

With that, he hurried away, and I felt sorry for delaying him.

I entered the practice room and found the youngest dancer, Han, sweeping the floor with a wet mop. She noticed me and told me Director Park was looking for me.

"Oh, really?" I said, looking back at the wall clock above the door. I wasn't late. Director Park looking for you in the early morning was never good. "How's her mood today?"

Han stopped sweeping, leaned toward me to get closer, and said, "The most red I have seen so far."

When Director Park was angry, her face was like a completely ripe strawberry. We could guess the kind of day it would be from her color.

"Thanks, Han. Is she in her office?"

"Yes, I would hurry."

I crossed the wet floor with an apology to Han and

turned backstage. When I opened the artificial leather door, Director Park was pacing back and forth in the office, her arms crossed.

"Close the door," she said, glancing at me, and plopped herself down on the sofa. Her ears were as red as Seunggyu's. "I was worried something like this would happen."

I put my black bag down next to the sofa. "What's wrong, Director Park?"

She leaned over slightly, without uncrossing her arms, and moved her face so close to mine that I could clearly see the wrinkles around her eyes. Maybe the rumor that her husband was having an affair with his coworker is true, I thought. Director Park was too young and too good a wife for that snaky old man. "Did you tell your story to Seunggyu?" she demanded.

I was surprised that our discussion had started with Seunggyu. "Yes…" I replied.

"He just stopped by here and asked me to tell him honestly about your background. He seemed so upset."

Was that why he came? Not for Jongmu, but for himself?

"Jia, I accepted you at the hotel because of Teacher Song. She told me about your family's history, and I took pity on you."

Director Park stood up and resumed pacing.

"Your boyfriend wanted to know everything, and he asked for some documents relating to you. Jia, he threatened me! He said his father's friend has a high position in the information bureau. I don't know what I'm supposed to do. I was so anxious whenever I saw you two together—I should have stopped you."

Director Park patted the back of her neck with the side of her hand. "Let's calm down first."

Pouring water from the yellow stainless-steel kettle, she guzzled a full cup. "Jia, try to convince Seunggyu not to hurt you; you've been together for a long time, and I'm sure he really loves you; that's why he feels so betrayed by you. He almost cried. But Jia, to him, your background is paramount. Don't trust love. Just beg him to forget about you and not to shake too much dust from your past—you've got to try and catch him as soon as possible."

I left her office quietly, with Han's anxious eyes trailing me. I had no idea where Seunggyu had gone, or if he really had a training session. Walking down the hall, I told myself, *Right, as Director Park said, I must find him and beg him to forgive me and restrain him from endangering my life.* But my legs were taking me back home.

Would he turn me in, send me to a political prison? It pained me that he had decided not to tell me how shocked he was. I couldn't forget his eyes at the hotel, darting away from mine.

I retired to my room for a long while.

Before sunset, I visited my friend and former colleague Jiyun. She had quit dancing at the hotel when she got married. Everything in her house was well organized—they still had furniture and a TV—and Jiyun's only worry was her long-unfulfilled desire for a baby. With a grin, she offered me dried anchovies on a plate. I had never seen such big anchovies; their eyeballs hung out of their sockets.

"It's strange…" she said. "What I missed the most after stopping work over there was Cook Kim's anchovy dishes. Remember? I always gave them to you. I never imagined myself sitting alone in the house, chewing on big dried anchovies. My husband brought them from China. Try them, Jia."

She picked up the biggest one and bit off the head. She gave me one, and I cut half of it off with my front teeth. I asked her how I might buy a black-market travel permit. I assumed she knew about such things, as her husband secretly bought and sold outside goods in the market.

"Everything is possible if you have money," Jiyun said, smiling. "I'll ask my husband. Where are you going?"

I didn't have any idea, but I had to make a plausible excuse. I felt the more remote the destination, the better.

"I have to go to Onsŏng. My aunt is there. She's dying and wants to see me before her death. I want to leave as soon as possible, even tomorrow is fine."

"I didn't know you had a relative so far away." Jiyun held her head at an angle. "Have you asked Seunggyu? He could definitely take you there. Then you wouldn't have to waste your money."

"No, and don't talk about it if he asks," I snapped. "He doesn't want me to go—he's worried. It's far away and her disease might be contagious. I'm keeping it a secret from him."

Jiyun nodded, lifting the little finger of her right hand to seal her silence. "What is her disease, then?"

At that time, paratyphoid fever and cholera were spreading all over the country. "She has cholera," I told her.

Making her round eyes even more round, Jiyun tilted her head to the other side. "Now? Isn't Onsŏng much colder than here? That's strange. Paratyphoid fever would make sense, but cholera? Now?"

I hesitated. In a panic, I said, "Actually, I don't remember exactly—maybe you're right. When I got the news from her husband, I was so shocked. The disease wasn't important."

"Right, I understand. I'm sorry, Jia. I'll urge my husband to hurry."

I gave Jiyun enough money for the travel permit, and two days later I had it in my hands. For 50 US dollars you could get any kind of document made. I was grateful to my customers at the souvenir store for their generous tips. Though Americans were our enemies, American currency was our friend when we were in danger. Runaways who had American currency could afford brokers, who would make the journey to China much safer.

Jiyun's husband kindly told me how to get to Onsŏng. I would have to travel to Hamhŭng first and then take a train to Onsŏng. There was a train from Pyongyang to Onsŏng, but it left infrequently and often broke down.

I had chosen Onsŏng, in the far northeast, because it was the farthest place from Pyongyang. Sinŭiju, just northwest of Pyongyang, would have been the fastest escape for me, but it had already become a popular route for runaways, and the army was waiting for them at the border. At least, that's what Seunggyu had confided in me.

I used the confidential information he gave me to abscond from him.

The night before I left, I looked slowly around my tiny home. It was the first place I could call my own, and I had tried to take care of it. Would I be able to return? I didn't want to leave the flat in disarray, so I wiped down every nook and corner.

There was nothing left for me here. I didn't own anything; I should have been the first to leave, not Sun or Gun.

I thought about Sunyoung for the first time in years. The look on her face and the sadness in her voice when we spoke in the restroom came back to me clearly; I could feel the pain in her heart, how lonely she must have been, and my heart filled with sadness. I wept that night, and watched the wall in the darkness, as Sunyoung might have done. I had always wondered whether she regretted her decision to follow her heart. The day she realized she had nothing and no one to lean on—how desperate she must have been!

Sunyoung's tragedy had changed my life; I couldn't deny it. Her bitter fate led me to close my eyes and ears. Like the other dancers, I felt that Sunyoung made a foolish decision, giving up the path of a comfortable life that had been offered to her to follow the passion that ultimately took her from me. Perhaps, with Seunggyu, I had hoped to choose the predictable life that Sunyoung had rejected. Listening to him, I had felt stable and safe; I felt that a happy life was possible.

How arrogant I had been! I had pretended to Seunggyu that my generous heart was the reason I felt sympathy for people who begged on the street, emboldened by the thought that I had been spared such wretchedness. The truth was that I was one of them, a trifling shell pushed by the waves this way and that. Seunggyu, when I saw him the last time at the hotel, recognized me for what I was.

The tears I cried that night weren't for Seunggyu, or for the memory of Sunyoung. I couldn't blame Seunggyu, after all, for betraying me, when I was the betrayer. I had the chance now to begin another journey in my life. I feared I would be unwelcome, yet again, in a new land, but I was resolved to fight.

Early the next morning, I tied the made-in-China lace-up shoes I had bought in the street market and set off for the Pyongyang train station. I was well layered in a thin white shirt and stockings, which I always wore for performances, two ivory sweaters, and thick brown pants. I wrapped my head in a dark-blue scarf and put on my oldest, worn-out coat. I tried to wear as much as possible, to keep my backpack light.

The streets were empty, and wind whistled through the alleys around my apartment. I got on my bicycle and rushed toward Ch'anggwang Street with my scarf pulled tight; I was afraid of being seen by anyone I knew. Crossing Taedong Bridge, Kaya Hotel and Pyongyang Station came into sight all at once. On any other day, I would have turned my bike to the right and headed for the hotel. But this wasn't any other day.

My head down, I made an abrupt left turn as the station grew larger, expanding beyond my field of vision. The Great Leader was smiling at me from the picture above the entrance, and my eyes stayed fixed on him; the larger his face grew, the more convinced I became that he was not actually looking at me, but rather up and into the far distance. That comforted me.

The station was already crowded with anxious travelers pacing the terminal. A conductor said there would not be a train to Hamhŭng or Onsŏng that day due to an engine problem; some would-be travelers turned back while others decided to wait out the delay in the station. I was afraid that Seunggyu would catch me after discovering my escape, and I needed to get out of Pyongyang. Grabbing the conductor's arm tightly, I asked him if there was no other way to get to Onsŏng. If I hadn't held him I felt he would have flown away without giving me an answer.

"You can catch a car ride on the street—just ask the driver to take you on board."

"Where can I catch those cars?"

"Go to any big street, you'll see the trucks. Try to the west, crossing the Pot'ong River."

I made my way to Sŏsŏng Street. Pedaling furiously, I headed northwest and passed over Sŏsŏng Bridge. The layers of clothing stuck to my body and I felt heavier and heavier. On the other side of the Pot'ong River, several groups of people were gathered along Pulkŭn Street, on the side that would take them toward Pot'onggang Station. Each group had five or six people, all waiting to catch cars, and all carrying big bags. Some had mirrors, rice, and salt bags; others even had televisions.

Leaving the bicycle on the grass next to the road, I joined the closest group. Whenever cars passed, we waved our hands, but were ignored. Finally, one man took money from his jacket and waved it around. Soon enough, a military car stopped with a screech and a soldier asked us where we wanted to go. The car was going to Kowŏn, in the far east. I knew there was a station there with trains to Onsŏng, so I got in without hesitating, along with seven others. After checking our travel permits, the soldiers took 300 won from each of us, no matter where we were going. That was about three months' salary for a factory laborer. Some people on the street were left behind because they wanted to go in other directions or didn't have enough money.

The car was extremely cold, and after taking a seat, everyone took a big, crumpled plastic bag out of their packs and wrapped it around themselves. Clearly, they knew what to expect. I could hear my own teeth chattering from the cold.

The man who had waved the money looked at me sideways and gave me a grin that exposed his dark-yellow gums. "You didn't bring a plastic bag?" he asked. He proudly adjusted his bag so that it covered his whole body from the neck down. His bag, unlike the others, had special holes for the head and arms. It seemed that he had cut the bag specifically for this purpose.

"No," I said, avoiding his eyes.

"It's spring, but it's still cold, and it'll be much colder when we climb up. Protecting yourself is the most important thing."

"I didn't know that," I said, pulling my knees to my chest.

He smiled and said, "I'll share mine for fifty won. Come inside."

He opened one arm and made space, pointing at it with his eyes. I didn't want to get close to a male stranger, but it was getting colder. A middle-aged woman with a snub nose sitting in front of me was watching the exchange and snapped at him, "How dare you take her money? Be generous."

She turned her head to me and said, "Come here. Let's share mine, it's big enough for two."

I grabbed my backpack and slid in next to her; warm air from her body hung inside the plastic bag. The man glared at the woman, but said nothing.

"Is it your first time catching a car?" she asked. Her snub nose was noticeably redder than other parts of her face.

"Yes." I rubbed my hands and blew on my frozen fingers.

"What that guy said is right. You should prepare. Otherwise, it's a perfect day to die from the cold."

The car rocked from side to side, bumping my tailbone hard against the seat, but eventually I fell asleep, letting go of the anxiety of the last few days. It was much better inside the plastic bag, sharing the heat of two bodies in that airtight space.

"Get up, get up."

When I opened my eyes, the others were already out of the car.

"Are we already in Kowŏn?" I asked the snub-nosed woman, who had taken off the plastic bag and was folding it.

"No, we're at Majŏn. The car broke down with a fourth of the way left to Kowŏn. They'll fix it, but they aren't sure how long it will take."

"What are we supposed to do? We already gave them money." I stood up, holding my backpack.

"You can take another car or wait until they fix it. But don't even think about getting your money back."

"What will you do?"

She swung her backpack, which was much bigger than mine, onto her back and clutched a pumpkin-shaped knapsack and a small mirror under her arm. "There is a street market close by—I'll go there and sell my goods. You can have a meal there and wait until they fix the car." She headed off to the right with nothing more to say.

As the passengers scattered, I asked a soldier who was smoking outside when he thought we'd be moving again, and he answered gruffly, "We don't know, not long, but not before night. Come back after dinner." The group of soldiers headed to the street market, leaving one to fix the car. He looked not more than 16 and seemed not to know what he was doing. I followed the group to the market.

So many smells emanated from the food stalls! My stomach gurgled at the smell of steamed sweet potatoes and egg breads and corn nuts fried in the pan. There were several groups of *kkotjebi* in the market. When they rushed past me, I had to breathe with my mouth, not my nose. I tried to find the people from the car. I saw the soldiers teasing a young woman in her food stall. She brought dishes to them with a coquettish smile, and some of them tried to touch her body. She didn't complain at all, but her face twisted as she got past them.

Two would be better than one, I thought, so I looked around the market for the snub-nosed woman. I accidentally bumped into a man coming from the other direction.

"Watch out!" he spat. "Are your eyes just for decoration?"

"Sorry," I muttered, lowering my head several times.

He grabbed my right arm. "If I was hurt just now, what would you do?"

"Sorry, I didn't mean it."

"How do I know you didn't mean it? Are you trying to mess with me?" he demanded, eying me skeptically.

"Sir, I was looking for my friend, and I was distracted. Forgive me."

I was scared by his reaction, and tried to wriggle my arm out of his grasp. He said, "Be careful next time," and rushed off.

I met the eyes of an old female merchant who was selling underwear in different colors. She looked at me first and then her eyes deliberately followed the path of the man. When I followed her glance, I saw him walking away with several men. I removed my backpack and saw that the bottom was half-torn and some of my clothes were pushing out through the hole. I scrambled to look inside; the gray sock where I put my money was gone. I had hidden my money in two socks and sewed them into the bottom of the backpack. I grabbed the torn part and ran in the direction he had gone, crying, "Thief, Thief! Catch him."

I pushed people aside in my dash to catch him, but he was gone. I spun around, crying out for help, but no one even looked at me; I was the only stranger in that place.

I returned to the car and found the boy soldier groaning.

"Can you fix it today?" I asked him.

"I'm trying." His face and shirt were soaked with sweat, even on the chilly day. I crouched down next to him as he worked.

My thoughts raced. Did I have to go back? No! I couldn't. Where should I go? I had left Pyongyang and lost half of my money within a few hours. What worse luck was waiting for me? I was as miserable as the boy soldier.

Several hours later, the group of soldiers came back sluggishly, picking their teeth with toothpicks. When they saw that the boy soldier still hadn't figured out how to repair the car, they kicked him several times. "You good-for-nothing!" they yelled, throwing two loaves of bread to him. He picked them up from the ground nimbly and devoured them without even dusting them off.

One of the soldiers took the tools from the boy soldier's hands, and 30 minutes later the engine of the car made a tumultuous sound. Only half the passengers had returned, and the soldiers didn't wait for the rest. The snub-nosed woman didn't return, so, for five won, I shared another woman's plastic bag.

11

Friendship with Kkotjebi

On arrival at Kowŏn Station early the next morning, I saw many kinds of people, and more *kkotjebi* than you'd find in the Pyongyang station and street market. They wandered around, begging for food from the crowds of people waiting for the train. Cigarette smoke and offensive smells greeted me everywhere. People with large bags grouped together—it made it easier to keep an eye on their belongings.

The railroad police patrolled the station wearing dark-green uniforms and expressionless faces, picking through people's bags with their fingers or with their thick, shiny truncheons. They looked about my age or a little older. Shifty-eyed men hung about like smoke in the air, stealing glances at people's bags. Young girls with worn-out clothes but thick makeup were everywhere, shouting, "Flower! Buy a flower!" But none held flowers. They only approached well-dressed, young and middle-aged men. Everything was unfamiliar, and everyone looked suspicious to me.

I wandered through the station but couldn't find a place to sit down. I suddenly felt someone was watching me carefully, following my movements, and I turned my head to find a small boy, dressed in tatters. Like other *kkotjebi,* his face was covered with dust. Under his hat, his eyes were twinkling, and as soon as they met mine, he walked directly to me, with a slight limp. That was my first encounter with Sangwon.

When he was close enough, he smiled and asked, "Do you have some food to share with me?"

I looked down at him skeptically, and he didn't take his eyes off me. Of course, I didn't have food to share. Everyone knew no one had food to share; the only way hungry people could survive was to steal, so this boy was either really bold or not so smart.

Setting out on my journey, I had made a firm resolution that I wouldn't share food; my own survival came first. I had just one loaf of bread and an ear of corn, and I needed to save what little money I had left. But Sangwon's blunt eyes, so steady on mine, made me hesitate. Or perhaps it was his limping leg that changed my mind.

I said, "I just have one piece of bread and one ear of corn."

I would have felt better if he had pretended to cry or grab my leg, but he just pouted with his lower lip, shrugged his shoulders, and said, "Okay. If you think that isn't enough for two people, that's fine. Have a good trip."

He was funny. His way of watching me and withdrawing without a fuss compounded my guilt.

As he turned around to walk away, I called after him.

"Wait… Maybe…we can make do with these for breakfast."

Sangwon turned back and smiled. "And then I might help you if it's your first time traveling," he said, winking. "I know where we can have a peaceful meal."

Like a gentleman escorting me, Sangwon gestured in the direction we should walk, strutting triumphantly, as though he had won something. His wiry body moved nimbly through the crowd.

He took me outside the station to an out-of-the-way corner that was chilly but still the perfect place for two people to sit side by side. Not too stinky either. He took his jacket off and shook it briefly. Laying it on the ground, he grinned, motioning for me to sit down. I felt the ground would be cleaner than his jacket, but I didn't rebuff the offer. Sangwon sat down next to me on the bare ground.

He smacked his lips as I took the food out of my bag, so I broke the bread in two and gave him the bigger half.

"I haven't seen bread for a long time. I eat watery gruel every day. That place only makes begging on the street look good." He stuffed himself with bread.

"Which place?" I asked.

"The nine-twenty-seven. I just got out of the nine-twenty-seven. Have you heard of it?" His big, round eyes turned to me; his cheeks bulged.

I had heard of the 927. The government tried to move beggars and people unable to make a living on their own to a specific place in each province, forcing them into abandoned buildings, usually former hotels. Because this system was instituted on September 27, 1997, it was called the 927. Supposedly it kept people from dying of hunger.

"Why didn't you stay there? At least you'd be fed regularly."

Sangwon's eyes bugged. "Are you kidding? Have you ever slept sitting up for several nights? That place doesn't protect people, it creates more problems. People die in there from diseases and hunger—we don't need that kind of protection." He ripped a piece of hard bread off with his teeth and ate it; he reminded me of a lion gnawing the meat off a bone.

"Why would you sleep sitting up?"

Sangwon stopped chewing and opened his mouth halfway. "You don't know anything. You're an alien, no wonder you stuck out."

He finished his bite and swallowed. "They put too many people in one small room. We all ate better on the outside."

When he spoke, he had to look up at me, and because his big hat covered his eyes, he took it off. His head was clean except for several scabs forming over his sores. He had no eyebrows or eyelashes; there was not one strand of hair on his face. He looked as if he had escaped from a Buddhist temple, not the 927.

"How long were you in there?" I asked, interrupting his eating again.

"Who knows? I gave up counting after seventeen days. Sitting in a corner, counting the days, made me more desperate. Anyway, I need to leave here as soon as possible. I don't want to end up back there."

"How did you run away?" I asked.

This time, he didn't raise his head to speak. "Through the window. I was stuck on the sixth floor. Some of the kids made a rope with our clothes and we ran away together. When the girl right after me was climbing down, the rope snapped. She fell and was dead on the spot. It could have been me."

I was shocked that such a small boy could talk about death with such a poker face.

Sangwon raised his head and his eyes fixed on my piece of bread. I hadn't started eating yet, so I handed it to him.

He shook his head. "I'm not going to eat my fill. I don't want to make my stomach expand." He patted his gut and smiled. "This guy is so sneaky. I give him enough food, but he always wants more. He's never completely satisfied, so I have to control him, or he'll control me. That's your share. I really appreciate what you gave me, but that's enough for today." He looked at me candidly, his eyes twinkling. Who could resist this face?

Sangwon pushed my hand back and urged me to eat the bread. I noticed that there were two stumps on his left hand where his fourth and fifth fingers should have been.

He saw me staring at his hand and raised both hands to show me. "I was lucky. That time, I was using my left hand and not my right."

He had tried to steal some food from a market stall while the owner wasn't paying attention, but just as Sangwon's hand approached the food, the owner caught sight of him and grabbed his knife. He just wanted to scare him, but Sangwon's two fingers were lopped off in an instant. The owner was as surprised as Sangwon, and they wept loudly together. Sangwon got the food from the owner, but his fingers were lost.

Sangwon told this as if it was someone else's story. He must have been used to it—he spoke so well. He looked about six or seven years old, but I guessed he was 11 or 12.

"Where are you going?" he asked.

I put a piece of bread in my mouth and chewed for a while. Could I trust this boy? Could I tell him I was running away? "I'm trying to get out of here," I said, almost to myself.

He watched me and kept his mouth shut for a while. At length, he said, "I got this disease when I was in the mountains."

Sangwon lifted one foot and removed his sock. All the toes were black from frostbite. He picked up a stone from the street, and before I could stop him, pounded the top of his foot with it. When I took the stone away from him, he smiled and said, "It's okay. I don't feel anything. They're completely dead. They aren't part of my body anymore." He put his sock back on.

"You should go see a doctor," I said, still staring at his foot.

"Oh, well. It's been long time. I got it when I crossed the river. Not a big deal."

Sangwon had guessed my plan. Most people came here hoping to cross the border; their large bags gave them away. Wandering around with a small backpack certainly made me look like a novice.

"I ran into pickpockets in a street market," I explained. "I didn't expect it. An old woman let me know my backpack was torn; I even didn't realize I had been robbed."

"Don't trust anybody here—even old women or soldiers. Oh, soldiers are the worst! They can do whatever they want. Don't even think about sitting next to them. Actually, you shouldn't have trusted me either."

He smiled as he said this, and I smiled back at him. How could I not trust this boy?

"This time of year is okay. In winter, it's easy to cross over because the river is frozen, but border control is much stricter. Summer is tougher—the water isn't as cold as in winter, but the river is high and the current is really fast, so border control isn't as strict. Young guys try in the summer.

Spring is the best time, because the water is low and not too cold. Now is still a little bit early. The ice must have melted, but the water will still be chilly. You should be prepared."

Sangwon put his hat back on. The hat was big and was peppered with cigarette burn-holes, but it looked really warm. I helped him find the front of the hat, and he pressed it down hard and said, "If you'll trust me one more time, we can go together."

I raised my eyebrows.

"We should get out of here as soon as possible," he continued. "I was heading to the border too."

I nodded, and he reached out his hand, smiling, and motioned me to do the same. He slapped my palm twice. "Okay. So we're comrades from now on. Did you buy a ticket?"

"Not yet. I don't know if I have enough money."

"How much do you have?"

I showed my money to Sangwon, my comrade. He counted it and said, "It looks okay, if the station didn't raise the fares." He stared pointedly at the badge on my chest. "But there is one way to make money." He handed my money back to me and asked, "Do you have a travel permit?"

"Here." I showed it to him, but he barely looked at it.

"Okay. Then it's much easier. What's your destination?"

"I haven't decided yet. I can go as far as Onsŏng with this card."

"Then let's go to Hoeryŏng. That's closer to the place where I usually stay in China."

We rose and walked behind the station. I saw a line of eight or nine people sitting down with their backs against the wall. Some leaned their heads on the person next to them, their eyes closed tight, while others gazed blankly in front of them, never blinking. Their skin was black, but it was different from the foreigners with black skin I'd seen at the hotel. Black spots covered their faces.

"Sangwon, don't you think those people look weird?" I poked his forearm.

Sangwon pulled me to his side. "You'd better not look. They're dead."

"No!" I shouted, in spite of myself, gripping his hand tightly.

"They all died of starvation, waiting there."

I looked again. The dead sat naturally and seemed to watch people as they passed. I shuddered with fear.

Inside the station, Sangwon elbowed his way through the crowd and pulled me along. We came to a man wearing a neat blue coat, standing with a small bag at his feet. The man lit a cigarette.

Sangwon walked up to him and pulled at his coat lightly. "Hello, sir. Did you find good things to buy over there?"

He looked down at Sangwon with annoyance and snapped, "Go away. I don't have any food."

"No, sir. That's not my business with you today. I have a badge to sell—how about a hundred and fifty won?"

The man sneered, "Where? Show it first. If you're lying, I'm going to break both your legs."

"See, I'm not lying." Sangwon pointed at my chest. The man's eyes moved to the badge and then up to my face, then to Sangwon and back to me.

"Are you willing to sell it?" he asked.

Sangwon glanced at me quickly and whispered, "You won't need that over there." Then he grinned and replied, "She will, for a hundred and fifty won. It's a nice one, with two leaders' faces on one badge. You can sell it at a good price to foreign travelers if they know it's really from North Korea."

The badge showed the faces of both Kim Il Sung and Kim Jong Il. Working at the hotel, I had had to wear it at all times. I couldn't believe I was selling it now. My chest without the badge—I hadn't even considered that possible.

The man examined the badge for a moment. "This one has too many scratches. One hundred won."

Sangwon immediately grabbed my hand and said, "Let's go, we can do much better. A badge with the two leaders is worth more."

The man seized Sangwon's shoulder and grimaced. "This *kkotjebi*—you know this place too well. Okay, a hundred and thirty won. Don't even think about more."

"Okay," Sangwon said, unpinning the badge from my chest. "Here. Give me the money."

The man pointed at me with his chin. "Is she your sister?"

"No, she is my mom," Sangwon replied instantly.

The man sneered, looking at me, "Are you kidding? Doesn't she sell flowers here?"

Sangwon growled back, "I said she's my mom. Of course she doesn't sell flowers." He grabbed my hand firmly and started to walk away.

The man shouted after us, "Let me know if you need help. I like your deaf-mute sister."

"That dirty-mouthed—" Sangwon swore without looking back at him.

"Why did he buy the badge?" I asked.

"He can sell it to foreign travelers in China as a souvenir. It's one of the most popular items there, actually. In China, you'll see Chinese selling North Korean items to foreign travelers everywhere. Here the badge is sacred, but there it's like a toy."

I felt empty, as if I had lost a part of my body.

As though reading my mind, Sangwon said, "It's not as important as our lives. It's just a souvenir now—what we *need* is money and food. You would have to throw it away as soon as you crossed the border, anyway. Keeping it would be dangerous." He pressed the money into my hand.

"By the way, why did he ask me whether I sell flowers?" I asked. "I have seen so many women shouting that they're selling flowers, but with no flowers to sell."

"What he asked was whether you'd sell your body to him."

My face turned red with anger. I turned and saw the man still standing there, leering.

"People find ways to survive," Sangwon said, pulling me away toward the ticket booth.

People were shouting over each other for tickets, pushing and pulling like waves beating on the seashore. It was far too crowded.

"Wait here for a moment," Sangwon said. "I'll buy a ticket, just give me the money." I looked at him for a second. He was just a *kkotjebi*, looking for food and stealing from others, but for some reason, I was sure he would come back.

He took my money and was sucked into the crowd. A few minutes passed. Did I even give him my travel permit? I checked my pocket, growing anxious. I stood on tiptoe and scanned the crowd—it was impossible to see him.

I was about to move away to look for him when I felt a tap on my back. I wheeled around to find Sangwon's beaming face. "I got it!" he cried, holding up the ticket.

I was ashamed to have doubted him. Looking him up and down, I asked, "Are you okay? Didn't you get hurt?"

"Sometimes a kid has an advantage," he said, handing me the ticket and the rest of the money. "I even gave them less than the fare. They didn't notice—they're just trying to get rid of as many people as possible."

While we walked to the platform, Sangwon warned me, "Even though you have a ticket, some crazy people will try to take your seat, so never leave it. Go to the restroom before getting on the train."

The train didn't come for four days, and in all that time we never left the platform. People complained that the trains never ran on schedule; the railway employees said fuel had run out. No one knew when the train might arrive. "Pretty soon," the train employees said, but they didn't know. Some people left to sleep in nearby inns. Women, young and old, walked around shouting, "Clean, warm house while you wait." I wouldn't go; I was afraid of missing the train. I bought food with the rest of my money, and we tried to eat as little as possible. Sangwon had a fever from the infection in his feet and was limping harder.

When the train finally arrived, it was as if war broke out. The distant whistle sounded and people jumped up and grabbed their bags, screaming and shouting; suddenly the whole place was alive with noise. The railroad police made us stand in one line, and a policeman made an announcement about civic morality. People who didn't follow the rules would be punished severely. Nobody listened.

As the policeman was finishing his announcement, a dozen men rushed the platform and scaled the gate. Hundreds of people pushed madly after them, and the railroad police were overwhelmed. Some thieves made the most of the opportunity, cutting the bottom of one unsuspecting man's bag with a knife and catching the corn that ran out in their own bag. A flock of *kkotjebi* rushed to get their share. Finally the man realized what was going on and bawled, "Damn these hoodlums," kicking the *kkotjebi*. They didn't budge until they had collected all the corn.

Railroad inspectors tried to check each passenger's ticket and travel permit, but it was useless. They beat anyone they found without proper documents, but the crowd pushed past them. They shouted, "You can't get on the train without a ticket and a card. We'll inspect you sons of bitches again on the train!"

People dashed for it anyway, some dropping off the train like falling leaves. Those who didn't have tickets or permits climbed up on the roof. The inspectors didn't care about them, saying they would all die of cold or electric shock.

Sangwon and I rushed to find a seat. Finding one, he said, "Sit here and don't move. Put your bag next to you. If people swear at you about having your backpack like that, don't listen. And don't be scared. If they scream, you yell at them too. Okay? I'll be right back."

I grabbed at his coat. "Where are you going?"

"I don't have a travel permit. I'll be back after the ticket inspectors pass this compartment."

I looked at him anxiously, but he winked and said, "Don't worry about me. I'm a professional. Be careful, some people seize this chance and steal other people's things. Don't take your eyes off the bag."

Sangwon slipped through the crowd and disappeared. His tiny body could fit anywhere.

The train gave several long whistles and the employees

shouted, "The train is leaving." Those stuck on the platform tried to climb in through broken windows. The train
started moving, and when I looked through the window,
I saw a man running alongside. He threw his bag inside
first and put his hand on the windowsill. His face distorted
with pain for an instant from the shards of glass in the sill,
but he didn't give up. When half his body was through the
window, a railroad policeman outside harshly grabbed him
from behind and yanked him down. I stuck my face out of
the window to see if he was okay, and he looked at me and
shouted, "My bag! My bag! Throw it back to me."

When I turned to find his bag, it wasn't his bag anymore. Passengers in the train were fighting over it. A big
soldier stood up and pushed away the others. He seized the
bag with a threatening look.

Nobody resisted as the soldier took the bag to his seat
and opened it. It was filled with bundles of clothes. I saw
some tattered gray pants tangled up with yellowish underwear.

The soldier angrily sifted through the bundles. "What
are these stinky things?" Then, opening a bundle, he found
machine parts. The soldier's companions grabbed the bag
and began rummaging through the clothes. Several more
machine parts came out. Then a rice ball, some fried tofu,
and bean sprouts—the owner's lunch.

The soldier said, "They are still hot. Let's take care of
these for him." Looking around intimidatingly, he and his
companions ate the food on the spot.

I was worried about Sangwon. The inspectors were
harsh to people who didn't have tickets, and I doubted his
age would make much difference.

Finally, a good while after the ticket inspectors had passed by, Sangwon reappeared, and we shared the seat. He fit in the space where my bag was, so I held my bag to my chest.

"Where did you hide?"

His hands were black with dust. He crowed, "Those people who work here aren't thorough enough to search between compartments. They don't care about *kkotjebi* anyway—we don't have anything for them. If we don't make trouble, they ignore us."

As we rode, Sangwon spoke about how he had lost his family. It's a common story in North Korea, and the reasons are always death by starvation or punishment by the government. He was an absolute orphan, but he smiled and said, "It's better this way; I don't have any pressure to take care of my family. Many *kkotjebi* have to beg for food for their parents or grandparents."

As an only son, Sangwon was adored by his hardworking parents. Both worked in a fertilizer factory in Hŭngnam, north of Kowŏn, and Sangwon remembered the chimneys shooting fat plumes of gray smoke up into the sky. The floods of 1995 and 1996 hit his hometown hard, and the polluted water brought disease and death. All the factories closed, and starving people started pillaging them for machine parts to sell on the black market or in China. Sangwon's parents were no exception. When they left him at home to travel to the border to sell some parts, their bus tumbled into a bloated waterway and was swallowed up. Sangwon heard the news of their deaths, but their bodies were never found.

Sangwon found himself alone in his house, with no idea what to do. For the first time he could play outside with abandon; nobody controlled him, and he didn't have to hear his mother's nagging. It was starvation, however, that came to control him. Soon he stopped going out. A neighbor said the government would take care of him, so he waited for them. When the government finally did pay Sangwon a visit, they said they would take his house, that it belonged to them. The only place he could go was the orphanage or a camp for children in similar situations.

The day before he was to depart for the orphanage, Sangwon heard there would be a public execution. A family was accused of eating human flesh. The family had been hungry for a long time, and they decided to sell their house and use the money to buy pork for soup. They went to a butcher's shop, bought the pork, made the soup, and ate well. Shortly thereafter, the police stormed into their house and arrested the entire family. The butcher had been selling human flesh, and they were all charged with murder, along with the butcher.

Out of curiosity, Sangwon walked to the public execution grounds. He found the street market completely closed. A crowd had gathered around the accused family and the butcher. A judge announced the charges as the crowd stood hushed in anticipation; only the family's sobbing could be heard. The judge asked the accused whether they acknowledged their crime, and a middle-aged man, who appeared to be the father, said they really didn't know what they had eaten, and begged for forgiveness. The judge declared they would not be excused for their crime. The youngest in the family, a boy, looked no older than six or seven, but the police said that he was 16—the minimum age to receive the death penalty. No one believed the police, but they dared not argue that he was only a boy. Perhaps they thought it would be better for the family to leave this world together.

Sangwon knew the boy was younger than he was. Their

eyes locked for the briefest moment, and he watched as the boy's eyes filled with fear. Policemen fastened the family members and the butcher to several long stakes and covered their mouths and eyes with towels. The family sobbed and pleaded for mercy. Moments later, the sound of simultaneous gunshots. The sobbing stopped at once.

People turned away and returned quietly to their houses. Some gathered in the street market to sell and buy goods again. Sangwon stood there for a while before heading home and packing his things in haste. He vowed never to feel fear such as he saw in the boy's eyes.

This was how Sangwon's journey began. By the time I met him, he had already crossed the border three times and been arrested three times in China. On the first occasion, the Chinese police caught him on the street and handed him over to North Korea. After the North Korean authority interrogated him, they simply warned him not to cross the border again and let him go. The second episode was the same. But, the third time, he ran into the same investigator and was taken to the 927.

Sangwon looked at me and giggled. "You know, when some people are arrested and have to be interrogated, they put their money inside their bodies so it won't be taken away by the investigators. Women put money wrapped in plastic bags in their...down there," he said, pointing between his legs. He continued, "Some people eat their bags of money or put it up their butts. If the police suspect them, they force people to eat food that causes diarrhea and then follow them to the restroom. Then the policemen search their shit to see if there is any money or valuables, like gold or silver rings and necklaces."

Sangwon taught me a song describing the *kkotjebi*'s life.

He said he learned it in the street market and that all the *kkotjebi* knew it. The lyrics were a dialogue between an old man and a *kkotjebi*.

Old man: *What is your name?*
Kkotjebi: *My name is jebi (swallow)*
O: *It sounds pretty*
K: *But, it is kkot–jebi (flower-swallow: beggar)*
O: *What do you eat?*
K: *I eat ori (duck)*
O: *You must be rich*
K: *But, I eat guksu-ori (noodle-duck: low quality noodles)*
O: *Where do you live?*
K: *I live in sudo (the capital)*
O: *You live in a nice place*
K: *But, it is ha-sudo (sewer)*

The train was pandemonium—slow and cold pandemonium. An icy wind came through broken windows, and in the dark before dawn, I saw a black lump drop from the sky and past my window.

I shook Sangwon. "Did you see that?" I asked, pointing outside. He was drowsy and said nothing.

A middle-aged woman in front of me spoke. "It's a dead person. Someone must have fallen asleep on top of the train and rolled off, or he died of electric shock up there and others pushed him off." I was stunned. Sangwon closed his eyes again, indifferent to her explanation. She continued, "That's not so bad compared to other things that happen on this train. If you see these scenes as often as we have, you won't care anymore either."

I fell asleep hugging Sangwon. Sleeping on the train was

brutal; the seat was so hard it hurt, and fleas and bedbugs bit me all over. Though vendors sold food at each station, I was afraid I would have to go to the restroom, so I ate only a little. Even the restroom was filled with people, and passengers gave up using the toilet in the restroom, doing their business between compartments instead. Shyness and shame no longer existed. Nobody cared. Nobody blamed others. People joked whenever someone relieved himself, saying, "That looks like it was a great meal!"

The train often stopped due to engine trouble; we were stuck at one station for a day and a half. The ticket inspectors came to check tickets at some stations, and passengers who didn't have tickets or travel permits sneaked out between the compartments and climbed to the top of the train. When the inspectors got to me, I stroked Sangwon's hair as he lay on my lap and told them he was my ill cousin and I was taking him to his mother in Hoeryŏng. Sangwon showed his spindly leg to the inspectors. They grimaced and turned their heads, then went on to check other people.

As the days passed, it seemed as if walking would have been faster than taking the train. I thought the journey would never end. Patience was a struggle. But, looking back, the train trip turned out to be the easiest leg of my journey.

12

To Cross the Border

As we approached the border in Hoeryŏng, the sun lit up the landscape, but the wind was so cold I huddled in my coat for warmth. Sangwon and I had left the train in the early morning and squatted down in the bushes near the border. There was no fence dividing the countries, and in the distance to the right, I could see a bridge connecting low mountains in each country. From a small hut on each side, two or three soldiers with guns on their shoulders came and went; if not for them, the border would have been invisible. I caught sight of a wide plain across the river, quiet and peaceful; I could even see houses and dogs. The mountains on the other side looked more luxuriant, more springlike. Sun might have gazed across the border from just the place where I stood.

Several soldiers in dark-green uniforms and broad-brimmed hats paced along the river, looking nervous.

"Today is a good time," Sangwon said, with a satisfied smile.

Four big military vans were crossing the bridge, coming from China.

"Those cars are coming from the Baekdu Mountains," Sangwon said, pointing casually.

The vans stopped in front of a white, four-story building, where several soldiers were waiting. A man wearing a lighter-green uniform got out of one of the vans, and a soldier approached him. They saluted each other and began talking. Other soldiers opened the back door of each van, and prisoners bound together by a thick rope emerged. The rope was tied around the first captive's hands, behind his back, and looped around the next captive's waist and hands. About ten people were chained together in that way. Some lowered their heads, others looked around. The soldiers kicked them; when one fell down, others in the same line staggered. The soldiers made each group of prisoners stand in one line. Then they pushed them into the white building.

"They'll be very busy, today," Sangwon said without taking his eyes from the scene.

"Who are they?"

"Those people were held in a detention center in China. The Chinese policemen are sending them under guard to this side. When I was caught, I was one of them too. There are so many today, more than a hundred…" Several children appeared to be Sangwon's age, and he tensed at the sight of them.

After everyone disappeared inside the building, the soldiers gathered together. Drivers got out of the cars and exchanged cigarettes.

"First, they must divide up the prisoners according to

where they will be sent," Sangwon said. "They'll start interrogating them tonight. Sooner or later, we'll hear screams from in there." He pointed with his chin toward the ugly old building.

I swallowed hard. Sensing my nerves, Sangwon patted my shoulder and said, "It's good luck for us, it means the lookout will be distracted tonight. Most of the soldiers will be in the building keeping watch over the prisoners."

Sangwon grabbed my coat lightly. "You are lucky. Tonight is a good night." He lowered himself further into the bushes, and his hat covered his eyes and nose so that I could only see his lips moving. "We have to be really careful, though, or we'll end up with them. Let's wait until sunset."

We lay down under the bushes for a while, and I heard the vans drive away. Pressing my whole body into the grass, I felt a sudden ache in my back and hips, and clenched my teeth, so as not to groan. After a while, the pain subsided. Several days of travel had taken a toll on me.

I tried to ignore the tremors shaking my body, but they wouldn't stop. When I looked up, I only saw Sangwon's glittering eyes looking down at me; the rest was dark. I tried to stand up, but Sangwon pushed my shoulders down, hard.

"Sh!" He covered his lips with his index finger. "Come here." He dropped to his knees and motioned for me to follow him. We were heading toward the river.

"You should swim as quietly and quickly as possible. Even if the soldiers discover us, don't stop, okay? Sometimes when they shout, "Stop," people feel they really ought to stop. Some old people actually stop in the middle of crossing the river. I'm not lying. So I'm warning you in advance:

Never, never stop. Don't even hesitate."

With a serious expression on his small face, he continued, "When we reach the other side, don't be relieved yet. Don't stop moving. Don't make too much noise there, either; there are also Chinese security guards trying to catch us. As soon as we find the bushes, we'll run for them and hide for a while."

When we reached the river, I froze and stared at what seemed like a dark floor spread out before me. The land on the other side looked much farther than I had estimated in the daylight.

Sangwon took off his clothes and rolled them up, putting them in his hat, which he held on the top of his head. His bones protruded from every angle of his body.

"Let's go."

Sangwon threw his body into the river while I took off my coat and shoes, stripping down to my underwear. Even surrounded by darkness, I couldn't help looking around for eyes spying on my half-naked body. I folded my clothes and shoes into my backpack, and tied the strings of the bag around my neck, to prevent the contents from getting wet.

With a throbbing heart, I stepped into the river. My teeth clenched hard and my body tingled with cold. The water only reached my navel. I looked at Sangwon. The water was almost at his shoulder.

He looked like a ghost, his body lost below the shoulders, creeping on a black floor. I thought I might be dying—the cold was cutting my flesh like a knife. Despite Sangwon's warning not to turn my head, I looked back at the white building and the water we had already crossed. The lump of the white building in the swallowing darkness looked even more run down; I swam for my life.

When we reached the far riverbank, I toppled out of the water and onto the ground. The cold wracking my body held me in place. My teeth were chattering, and Sangwon gestured for me to bite down on the string of my backpack. There was no time to rest, so we stumbled to some nearby bushes and I sprawled out flat on the ground. I couldn't think; I couldn't even hold up my head. I closed my eyes tight. Straining my ears, I tried to catch some sound, but it was deathly quiet. The cold wind made my water-soaked clothes even colder, and I held Sangwon's hand tightly. I was relying on the strength of a boy with such small shoulders. He nudged my hand and gestured to me to put on all of my dry clothes, just as he was doing; there was no shame or shyness left. I slipped off my undergarments and changed into dry clothes, but the chill had settled into my body for good. Again, we waited in the bushes without stirring.

I don't know how much time passed. Sometime later, in the darkness, Sangwon pulled me by the hand and we stole deeper into the strange, new land.

13

Life Underground

We moved at night and hid under bushes in the daytime, walking through the mountains on sequestered roads. We were afraid of running into wild animals, but there was no choice. Before the sun rose, we would find some tall grass and try to sleep; my mind could never completely rest, despite my body's utter exhaustion. Sangwon complained that walking through the mountains took two or three times longer than using the regular road. I prayed not to be detected no matter how long it took.

I wondered what was happening back in Pyongyang; had Director Park and Seunggyu discovered my disappearance? I hoped I hadn't caused trouble for Director Park.

It didn't feel as if the ground I was stepping on was that of a different country. The grass, rocks, trees, and sky were the same as those I knew in North Korea. Sometimes, from the bushes, we saw farmers or houses in the distance; the houses had exactly the same shape as ours, and the farmers' faces and clothes didn't seem so different from mine. I kept reminding myself, I'm in a different place now. All of this is new.

Sangwon and I were so afraid, we barely talked as we walked. Sometimes we gestured to each other or whispered, "Don't worry." That was all we could do. The food we had brought was already gone, and we needed to preserve our energy. Sangwon would pull the bark from a certain kind of tree and strip off the white insides for us to chew. Chewing made the wood softer; eventually I could taste some flavor, and the bark kept us from starving.

The deeper we got into the mountains, the safer we felt. Sangwon explained that we were going to the cave he stayed in whenever he crossed the river. He said he heard people had made the cave decades ago as a dugout to hide from a Japanese attack. There were several such dugouts deep in the mountains where people like us stayed.

After an arduous climb, we finally reached the cave. From the outside, you couldn't tell it was a cave. There was a small mound covered with tall weeds—passersby would guess it was just an unattended grave—but behind the weeds was a round hole in the rock, just large enough for an adult to crawl through. The deeper in we crept, the wider the cavity became. Sangwon said it was safe, but in the dim light I could feel my pupils growing, along with my fearfulness.

Dimly, I could see that a few people were already seated inside the cave. They didn't even look at us—they were unsurprised by strangers. We found a vacant place, and an old woman lying next to it propped herself up on her elbows. "Aren't you Sangwon?" she asked.

Sangwon beamed. "Grandmother! I didn't expect to find you here."

Weakly, she tried to grasp Sangwon's hand. "I was in another town, but I got back a week ago," she said.

Sangwon scrutinized her. "What happened to you? Are you okay?"

She shook her head. "I got hit by a car, crossing the street, and ran away with all my might. I was afraid the police would catch me. There was no place to rest safely in the town, so I came back here."

Sangwon stooped over her tenderly. "How did you climb the mountain in your condition?" He rubbed her shoulder with concern.

She smiled weakly. "It's okay. It's not serious, I'm just old. Old people are slower to recover than you kids—I'll be fine in a few days."

Glancing quickly at me, she said to Sangwon, "She's a new face."

Sangwon answered delightedly, "She's my mom."

I didn't say anything, but smiled at her and at Sangwon in turn.

Grandmother didn't ask anything more; she lay down again and muttered to herself, "Helping each other is good. Anyway, it's a long road to survive here."

As night fell outside, people returned to the cave one by one. Some recognized Sangwon and said hello, others didn't know him and didn't care. "Is it your first time?" they asked, or, "Do you have some money to exchange for food?"

Quietly, Sangwon explained to me how the people in the cave lived. When the sun came up, some would go to town to work or to beg for food or money, while others would climb into the mountains to look for food.

The cave seemed to be about a hundred meters deep, and it stayed cold no matter how warm it was outside. To be safe, we couldn't start a fire, so plastic bags kept us warm as we slept.

Every night, two people took turns acting as lookouts in front of the cave. If some people staying in the cave didn't show up for a night or two, it meant that they were arrested on the outside, or had moved on to another place.

We were quiet and kept to ourselves. Some people cooked together, others cooked separately. They had learned to cook rice in a special way in order not to be caught by the police; it was called "cooking rice underground." You put uncooked rice in a plastic bag with water or snow, and bury it, and then light a fire on the ground with branches of bush clover. This was one of the strategies people had learned in their guerilla training, so living in the mountains wasn't difficult for them. We exchanged information about how to survive. What the men had learned from their mandatory ten years of military duty in the service of the nation was now extending our lives outside of it.

The night Sangwon and I arrived, both of us collapsed. His leg swelled so that he couldn't walk. His fever spiked. We slept for several days like dead people.

Three or four days must have passed. We were able to get some food from the others, and at least the seclusion made me feel safe.

Early one morning, Sangwon woke me up and said, "Sister, I'll go to town today."

I looked around and saw that some people were already preparing to go out. I thought I should stop him. "Not yet, Sangwon, your leg needs more rest." I rubbed his calf. It was still swollen, and bruises covered his thigh.

"No—see?" He rose to his feet and swiftly walked back and forth, wobbling a little bit. His leg actually looked much better. "I don't have any problem walking now," he insisted. "I know my body, I'm really much better. I'll bring some food today—we also owe food to the ones who shared with us."

I got halfway up and said, "I'll go with you."

He pushed me back down. "You need to rest another day or two. Then we'll go to town together and I'll show you around. I'm going to get some garlic in town—if you chew three raw garlic cloves three times a day, your cold will go away."

Sangwon followed others out of the cave, and I lay down again and looked up at the ceiling. I felt relieved. If I hadn't met that small boy, what would have happened to me?

In the afternoon, Grandmother asked me to go find something we could eat in the mountains. She seemed to have recovered from her injuries.

"Sangwon will bring some food," she said. "He's really smart. In the town, he even has his regular fans who give food or money only to him."

I was feeling much better, and I thought Sangwon would be happy if I too found some vegetables or fruits to eat. I put our belongings away in the corner and prepared to leave.

Following several women who remained, I crawled out through the mouth of the cave and emerged into blinding sunshine. I squinted instinctively, but the warmth felt so good it seemed to flow through me. As my eyes adjusted, I felt the cool air. I glanced up at the sky for a second and then back at the mouth of the cave. From the outside you would never notice the entrance; it was the perfect place for us to hide.

I turned and found a strange man staring at me, with

several others behind him. There was a brief silence, and then he said something I couldn't understand.

The women behind me in the cave cried out, "Run away, run away! The Chinese police have come!"

The strangers rushed toward us. The man who had stared at me tried to grab me. I pushed him and ran, jumping into the nearest bushes. Resting for several days inside the cave had made my legs weak, and I stumbled as I tried to pick up speed. Screams echoed behind me. Sangwon always said I should run without looking back, so I ran straight ahead. I felt my chest expanding unbearably. I pulled back my head to lessen the pressure on my chest, but I couldn't breathe. I felt as if I was dying, yet I ran and ran. When I could run no farther, I tumbled onto the ground.

Exhausted and out of breath, I grabbed on to some weeds and firmly closed my eyes. If they find me, they will beat me, I thought. If they try to stand me up, I won't move at all. This place will be my grave. I felt gooseflesh all over my back. I was too scared to move, even to turn my head.

I remembered the night my sister and I were walking in the forest. We were startled and ran home, terrified that something was following us. My grandfather had always warned us not to be outside so late. He frightened us, telling us that ghosts might catch us from behind and have us for dinner. In the years I had spent dancing for the festival and working at the hotel, the memory of my youth in the mountains had faded. Sometimes I felt it was another lifetime, or perhaps only a dream. But all at once the terror of that night with my sister returned. I squeezed the weeds with all my might, as I had my sister's hand.

I kept myself flat on the ground for many minutes, but nothing happened. No yelling voices, no footsteps. After a while, I turned my head and felt a tranquil wind against my cheek. Above me I saw the wide sky, the trees, the flying leaves. The sun was blazing. I breathed slowly, watching the sky. A swarm of large dragonflies flitted about. The grass was silent, save for the pounding of my heart.

It took me hours to return the way I had run. I found footprints where I had trampled the grass, but they soon disappeared. I looked for familiar landmarks, but I hadn't been outside the cave since my arrival. I was lost. It was still day, but in the mountains nobody could guess when darkness would fall. I hoped I wasn't too far from the cave.

I looked around me. The wind was chilly in the mountains, but I felt spring had arrived in earnest. Everywhere the trees were green with new growth. I tried to walk in a straight line, but I couldn't be sure I was going the right way. I prayed I might run into someone returning from town, but I encountered no one. I heard the sound of water flowing in the distance.

Eventually, the sky turned completely dark, and I couldn't see two paces in front of me. I wondered if I should stop for the night. I stood still, afraid to move and afraid not to move.

So many people escaped to China only to land in more trouble than before, spending every moment in fear, worrying for their safety. The darkness of the mountains engulfed me. What am I looking for in this strange place? I wondered. Where are my friends?

Each question led to another. My strength and desire were gone. I didn't have a destination. Other people had goals. Some people, after getting to China, tried desperately to travel onward to other, safer countries. Others wanted to return to North Korea with money and food. What were my goals? Right now I was looking for the cave. But after that? What do I seek here?

My whole life, I had been a runaway: I had slipped away from my real family; I'd run away from myself until I reached what seemed like the darkest corner of the Earth.

Before escaping to China, I had reasoned that class status was unimportant in China, that I would not be judged here. I wouldn't have to feel the guilt of shouting the daily slogans at the hotel before the Great Leader's picture, pretending to be an upright citizen. But now, despair overwhelmed me. I was not welcome here either. In China I am just another kind of criminal, wandering around in the darkness and running away in fear of being caught. Will there ever be a happy outcome to my life? If I were to die here, no one would know.

A lump of anger burst in my chest. My parents had broken the rules, and that made me a criminal too, but what did they do that was so bad? I thought of the dancers at the hotel. I was crazy with jealousy, imagining their happy faces, their happy stories with their families. Now I could be honest with myself: I was madly envious. I was born unwelcome. Struggling like this seemed pointless. My birth was unwelcome, but at least my death would be welcome—to me, anyhow. My body lay crumpled on the grass; perhaps this was my destiny. I felt like the seven-year-old girl who was abandoned in the forest, hoping Uncle Shin would find her. But the scared woman lying in the grass now didn't have anything or anyone.

At that moment, I heard the sound of repeated whistling. It didn't sound like an animal. It was getting closer, and I stood up abruptly and whistled back. The whistling stopped; only silence from the other side. Was it human? Who was it? I crept down again and lay still in the grass. It could be a friend, but it could be an enemy. Another whistle, closer this time. Looking in the direction of the sound, I could see a black figure illuminated slightly by the stars.

I grabbed the long branch that I had used to beat a path.

The figure closed in on me, whistling again, then spoke quietly. "Jia... Are you Jia?" It was a man's voice, a strange voice, but he knew my name.

I swung the branch at him. I had nothing to lose anymore. "Right here! Who are you?"

He stopped. "Where are you?"

I stood up and approached him; his eyes gleamed in the darkness. It was a man who had been staying in the cave, a man who knew Sangwon. I remembered his face.

He was relieved. "Oh! You were here. You don't know how Sangwon worried about you. Come on, I'll take you back."

The Chinese police had captured several escapees outside the cave that day, most of them old people incapable of running away. When Sangwon returned and saw that I wasn't there, he became frightened. A woman who had watched the struggle with the policemen reassured Sangwon that I wasn't one of those who were captured. Sangwon wanted to find me, but this man stopped him and said he would look for me instead. He knew Sangwon couldn't find me with his injured leg.

When we arrived back at the cave, Sangwon sprang to his feet, staring at me with relief. I patted his bare head and said, "I ran straight ahead, without looking back, the way you taught me." We sat in silence as he picked the weeds from my clothes. There were tears in his eyes.

I decided not to dwell any further on the questions that had arisen outside in the dark. Sangwon, too, had wandered in darkness. Despite his determination and optimism, I could see fear and despair in his eyes. He always told me we would only be partners until we found a safe place, but he was afraid of losing me and being alone. He needed someone he could lean on, too. He needed someone to give him a reason to struggle, to keep hope alive. Just as dancing had become my purpose after being rejected by my grandparents at the orphanage, I was what Sangwon needed now. I didn't want to break his heart; I knew I couldn't disappoint him. We were not merely partners for survival. We gave each other hope.

Grandmother's place in the cave was empty. No sooner had her wounds healed than she had fallen victim to an even greater disaster.

14

Trust and Distrust

There were regular visitors to the cave whom nobody welcomed. They called themselves intermediaries; they said they could help us start new lives, that they knew all the good jobs in China. But no one trusted them. They were only nice to the young women; when they came to the cave, they looked around for new faces. After Sangwon and I had been there for a week, three of them showed up.

"How's everything?" one asked.

They lounged about the cave, checking each person's face to see who was new. People just sat quietly or nodded their heads to the uninvited guests. The only reason they came was to persuade young women to go to town with them; women and children could get more food in town than a man could. If the men in the cave told them a woman didn't want to go with them, the strangers couldn't force her, but if she wanted to leave with them, nobody could stop her. We all knew they could report us to the police anytime they wished.

Ignoring the visitors, I hugged Sangwon and pretended to sleep. One of them spotted us, however, and drew near. He nudged Sangwon in the ribs and said, "Hey, Sangwon. You came back. We wondered if you were okay. We haven't seen you for a long time. Is your leg any better?"

He made Sangwon stand up. "Who is this woman?" he asked. "We haven't seen her before, right?"

He looked around at the others, but they kept their heads lowered. Moving his face close to mine, he called loudly to his friends, "Hey, check out the new face!"

The other men approached and Sangwon glared at them, shouting, "She's my mom. Nothing interesting to you guys."

They pushed Sangwon away and dragged me to my feet. "Sangwon, we know your mom is dead. Sorry about that," the man said. He snickered.

The strangers watched my face intently. "She looks too young to be your mom, anyway," one of them said.

They surrounded me. One of them leered, "This place isn't so comfortable for you. Is it, young lady?" He sat down and grabbed my hand. "You haven't experienced the harsh world yet. Your white hands and face show it."

Sangwon barked at them, "Don't touch her. I said she's my mom."

They glared at Sangwon and he glowered back, then looked around the cave, appealing to others. There was Kangmin, who had a robust physique; he was the one who had found me, he always helped old people and children.

Kangmin approached the man and said, "They're like

mother and son, and we treat them that way, whether it's true or not."

The man who had grabbed my hand stood up and threw Kangmin a furious look. "Why didn't you report her to us? That was our deal, wasn't it? We give you guys a nest, provide jobs for some of you, and don't give you away to the police."

Kangmin lowered his head and said, "Sorry, but she and Sangwon really are like mother and son. She won't leave without him."

The man came close to me again and sat down. "But she has a right to listen to what a good world we can show her," he said, with a dirty smile. "And what a nice job she can get."

The intermediaries' job was selling women. As illegals on the Chinese side of the border, North Korean women found that their options were limited. Men could work on farms or at construction sites for a third or half the wages of legal laborers; children and the elderly could beg on the street. What could women do?

The man was watching me very carefully. "What did you do over there? You must have had a nice job as a dancer or artist. I can tell."

I couldn't stand him any longer and sprang to my feet. "I'm not leaving this place, so don't waste your time."

He stood up too and smiled. "Why do you want to live in a place that looks like a bomb hit it? It's cold, and you might be captured and sent home at any moment. We are not bullying you; we can provide security and a happy life. Think about it: you're young and pretty, all kinds of opportunities await you out there, but if you reject them, you get nothing."

I turned my back to them and took Sangwon's hand, leading him to the other side of the cave.

The man didn't follow us, but he spoke loudly so everyone else could hear. "We won't force you, just think about it. You want to take care of Sangwon. Right? You can make money to cure his rotten leg, and help him get a regular education. Think about how pathetic he is. He'll lose his leg pretty soon. After a while, his whole body may rot."

Sangwon growled at them, like an animal.

The man put his hands in his pockets and whistled to his friends to leave. "You can think about it until the next time. Bye, Sangwon. Take care of that leg."

As the men departed, people exhaled sighs of relief. I was frightened; they said they didn't force people, but it was clearly a threat. I looked at Sangwon's leg, the man's suggestion ringing in my head.

Sangwon looked at me angrily and said, "Don't even think about it. Don't trust them, they are scoundrels. Everything they say is pure trash. They work for their own greedy stomachs, not for us. They sell women every day."

I rested my hand on his head and assured Sangwon I wasn't taken in by their suggestion. But I was concerned as I looked around the cave. It was a temporary shelter for all of us. None of us knew where we could go or how we would make a living elsewhere, but we also knew the cave wasn't safe. Sangwon and I had made plans to move on in a matter of weeks. We needed more time to get over our physical problems. Sangwon suggested we go to a big city, where it would be easier to hide our identities and to adjust. We decided to depend on each other until it was best to separate. His leg was looking better as the weather warmed up, but the man's warning that Sangwon's body would fall apart stayed with me.

Several days later, the men returned early in the morning, before anyone had left for town. They didn't harass me, but I didn't like their smiles as they shuffled around, full of entitlement.

One asked me, "How is it living here?"

I didn't respond.

"Tell me what you did over there." He came closer.

"You didn't run away just because of hunger—did you commit a crime? Do you have some secret you can't tell us?" He sat in front of me. I took a step back and averted my face.

Sangwon, who had just awoken, tried to sit up. I patted his shoulder and said to the man, "It's none of your business."

"I know that," the intruder said. "I'm just asking. I want to help you."

"I can help myself."

Another of the men shouted to him, "Why do you bother her? Come over here."

A woman who had arrived at the cave when we did was speaking to the men privately. One of them touched her shoulder and said, "That's a good decision. You won't regret it." Then they took her to a corner of the cave and spoke to her in a low voice; she nodded and went back to her place. She quietly packed her belongings and sat down, avoiding the eyes of the people watching her. She told her story to the woman who slept next to her.

She had crossed the border carrying her two-year-old daughter on her back. She said that as she was crossing the river, something yanked on her hair, but she didn't turn back. After she got across, she took her daughter down off her back and found that she was dead. The thing pulling on her hair was her drowning daughter. When she arrived at the cave, her spirits were low. She was a gazelle-eyed woman who seemed unable to endure the hardship. She spent her days in silence, watching the ceiling. Sometimes, at night, we could hear her muffled crying. No one could console her.

The cave dwellers were used to such tragedies; many of them had similar stories themselves. They tried to ignore her and sleep, as they were loath to be reminded of their own sadness.

In the days that followed, people went back to their own business, working on the outside and trying to save for their futures. Nobody knew how much money others kept and what kind of food they had in their backpacks. We all had our secret hiding places. It was the strictest rule not to touch other people's belongings.

The morning after the unwelcome visitors left, as people were getting ready to leave for the day, Kangmin called to Sangwon, "Did you know there is a party in town today?"

As soon as Sangwon heard, he sprang to his feet eagerly. "Really? Are you sure? I haven't heard that."

"Today is that grandfather's birthday—in the Zhang family. I'm sure you can get a lot of food; the old guy especially likes you, doesn't he?" Kangmin smiled.

Sangwon looked doubtful. "He didn't mention it when I stopped by his house last week—that's unlike him."

Bangmu, who was always with Kangmin, spoke up, "He's an old guy. At his age it is easy to forget things. Why don't you go? I'm sure they've started the party by now."

Sangwon was already putting his clothes on as he spoke. "Let's go. We can get a lot of food." He drew me by the arm.

Bangmu put his hand on Sangwon's shoulder and said, "Why don't you go with me? She can't carry a lot of food, but I can help you. We'll bring back a load of food and have a party here. In the meantime, Kangmin and Jia can find bush clover so we can cook rice and scorched rice water."

Sangwon grabbed his coat, "Let's go then. Sister, I will be back soon. Try to find as much clover as possible. I'm going to bring a lot of food so all of us can eat to our hearts' content." He proudly tapped his chest.

They left at a trot. Sangwon looked like a little squirrel; his limping was a piteous sight.

Watching him leave, Kangmin said from behind me, "Let's go pick some branches. I know where to find bush clover."

Kangmin walked really fast. I liked him; he never said much, but everyone trusted him. People in the cave didn't talk about their past lives. Sangwon said people used to speak freely about their work back home, and why they had decided to cross the river. But then some were arrested by the North Korean police, and they divulged other people's secrets to lessen their punishment. After that, people exchanged warm greetings in the cave, but no one shared their past.

As we climbed down the mountain, however, Kangmin told me about himself. He said he had to support his seven brothers and sisters in North Korea. He was a soldier who had firmly trusted in communism and still believed the ideology. He had a nine-year-old brother who was born blind but was full of energy and ambition. One day, his brother disappeared—he went outside by himself and was so hungry he ate some poisonous grass without realizing it. After that, he couldn't speak or hear at all; he lost every connection to the world. That's when Kangmin had decided to cross the border, in the hope of saving some money and eventually bringing his brothers and sisters back with him to China.

Suddenly, he stopped and looked around.

"Is this the place where we can find bush clover?" I asked.

"Yeah. I think so…hold on."

He whistled. A moment later, someone whistled back.

The three men who had visited the cave earlier suddenly appeared through the bushes. They approached us. One smiled and said, "Oh, what a coincidence! Sangwon's young mother!"

With them was a woman I hadn't seen before. She wore thick makeup. Her long hair, parted in the middle, hung down to her waist, and her tiny, button-shaped eyes contrasted sharply with her long eyebrows, which swept back to her hairline.

She walked up to me, ahead of the men. "Is this the girl?" she asked.

The man who had threatened me walked up behind her. "Right. What do you think?"

"It could be big money," she answered.

"See? I told you. It was worth the trip, right?"

He laughed, satisfied. She gazed into my face and then eyed me from top to bottom as she walked around me.

"You guys did a good job this time."

My head was reeling. I turned to Kangmin, who was standing apart from us. His eyes were evasive. He murmured, "It won't be so bad for you—it will be better than this place. I'm doing this for you…and for my brothers and sisters. Please remember that you are saving several lives. I promise I'll take care of Sangwon." His voice wobbled.

Sometimes, in life, people cross unexpectedly into a different world. For me, such a crossing happened in that moment. I had often imagined how I would react to difficult situations, how I would handle myself, whether I would be brave or meek. But a scenario such as this had not figured into my wildest speculations.

I was frozen, and there was no sound in my throat. I tried to reach for something familiar; I turned to Kangmin's face one more time, but he would not meet my eyes.

Someone tossed a lump wrapped in newspaper to him. "That's for you and Bangmu."

Kangmin didn't pick it up right away. Like me, he was frozen. I wanted to ask him what was going on—perhaps he could explain it all and everything would be resolved. Surely there had been a mistake. I took a step toward him, but one of the men grabbed my arm and the strange woman covered my mouth and nose with a white cloth. I saw Kangmin's face lose focus, and again I tried to reach out my hand. The last thing I saw was his cold, hollow eyes. I struggled to keep them in sight, fighting to keep my eyelids open, but his eyes swirled and grew bigger until they were consuming my whole body. I passed out.

Part 4

15

That Woman

M ore than 20 women lived in the large room where I was dumped. Huge men patrolled the halls to keep us inside. Occasionally, one of the women looked pitifully at me and said, "Time will solve everything." There were no bruises on my skin, but my muscles and bones ached. One of the thugs brought me food twice a day.

I lay facedown in a corner of the room that first night, wishing I could close my eyes forever, wishing myself back to the cave.

When I woke up, I was inside a large car, my body crumpled into the back seat, my hands and legs tied together with rope. Looking behind me, I found the face of the woman whose baby had drowned in the river. She smiled awkwardly at me; the dimples on both sides of her chin carved themselves into deep, bashful crescents.

One of the men noticed that I was awake and patted my shoulder. "If you'd been more like her, we wouldn't have had to treat you so harshly," he said. "It's okay now. Take it easy—it's a long trip. If you're not comfortable, let me know, and I can loosen the rope. Or I can tie your hands and legs separately."

I tried to remember what had happened. I recalled Kangmin taking me to a hill to find clover branches; he was unusually talkative that day. We were supposed to have a party in the cave. And then we ran into those people, and here I was stuck in a strange car. I thought about Sangwon. He must be back from town by now—he must be looking for me.

"How long did I sleep?" I asked the deep-dimpled woman. She answered cautiously, "A long time... We thought you might be dead." The man chimed in, "You slept for more than ten hours. I didn't know that medicine was so powerful." He snickered.

"Where am I going? What did you do to me?" My anger and the cigarette smoke inside the car drew dry coughs from my throat.

"We already told you several times we want to introduce you to a better world," the man said. "We felt sorry for you. You'll see how exciting our place is, how much better life is, and if you don't like it, you can leave. Look at her—" He smoothed the deep-dimpled woman's hair, and she lowered her head. "See how smart she is! You two should look to each other. From now on, we're a family. Welcome to our family." He looked much younger than Kangmin; the pimples on his neck turned dark pink with excitement. One of the other men began snickering. They all had the same army hairstyle, shiny black leather jacket, and loose thin gray pants.

A woman sitting next to the driver in the front seat turned back and warned him, "Save your breath, you talk too much. I have a headache now. Why do you chatter on like a housewife? Act like a man!" It was the woman who had accosted me on the hill when I was with Kangmin. She was wearing sunglasses even inside the car, but I recognized her.

I thought it must be past midnight, but when someone lowered the window to throw out a cigarette butt, night became day. Fields, mountains, houses, and trees appeared and disappeared quickly.

Kangmin's words echoed in my brain; it had all been set up. Could he really believe this was best for me? Would he really take care of Sangwon? Sangwon always said he wanted to grow up to be like Kangmin. He joked that he'd be much cooler than Kangmin, but never as hairy.

I wondered how Kangmin would explain my sudden disappearance to him.

"We have new sisters here!"

After several hours of driving, we were let out of the car into a narrow alley stinking of trash and food. The area was dense with buildings, and we were apparently behind one of them. Taking a bunch of keys from her handbag, the woman I saw on the hill opened a small door, and two men dragged us into a five-story brown building. Inside, it was dark and quiet; our footsteps reverberated through the hallway.

As soon as we were let in, without a single word the woman left. The men pushed us into the elevator and took us to a room on the top floor, announcing our arrival to its occupants.

Most of the other women were sleeping, and those who weren't didn't even look up. One of the men behind us said, "Get some rest. We'll call you later." He looked around the room and spoke loudly, "Hey, take care of these two—they don't know anything about this place. Treat them like younger sisters."

No one answered, but then he didn't wait for a reply. The door closed and I heard his footsteps tapping down the hall.

A woman with a husky voice pointed her chin in our direction and muttered, "Don't forget to take your shoes off." There was not enough space to lie down, so we sat right next to the door. The woman with the husky voice advised, "Rest now, while you can. You'll be busy soon enough."

She had big, flat, flesh-colored bandages on both eyebrows. I shot a sidelong glance at them, and she turned toward me, thrusting her face close to mine.

"I can take these off today," she said. She pointed to her right eyebrow with her index finger.

"What happened to your eyebrows? Were you hurt?" I asked, leaning away from her face, which had come too near to mine.

She sat up and opened her small black bag. "No. I had plastic surgery. Actually, I got my eyebrows tattooed once several years ago, because drawing eyebrows on every day was too much of a hassle. They looked good at first, but then they began to spread out, like hairy bugs. So gross! I couldn't stand them anymore. So, a week ago, a plastic surgeon cut the fleshiness under my eyebrows a little bit. Today I can take these bandages off. Isn't that fast? The technology for cosmetic surgery is getting better. If you want to use the hospital, let me know. It's so cheap and so professional. But there is a long wait, even for my simple surgery; I waited for two months."

I listened to her blankly. She looked a little bit older than the other women there, owing mainly to her high, protruding cheekbones. She smiled and unpeeled part of the bandage on the right eyebrow to show me. "See! It looks fine. Even the wrinkles above my eyes are gone after cutting out that useless flesh. I couldn't wait a week, I was always checking. It looks even better than yesterday."

I blinked. There was really nothing in the place where her eyebrow should have been. Instead, I saw a scar stitched with a thread. It scared me, but I said, "Yes. It looks fine. But it would be strange not to have eyebrows."

She replaced the bandage and looked at herself in the small mirror of her compact. "It's okay. I'll tattoo them on again. But a different shape than I had before. I was sick of those." She picked up a magazine and murmured, "I'm searching for suitable eyebrows. Apparently, crescent eyebrows are in style right now."

Soon, I noticed that every woman's face around the room looked artificial. They spent so much time looking at themselves in their mirrors. Some of the women spoke Korean, and I could tell from their accents that they were from North Korea. I knew they'd noticed mine too, though they gave no sign. Others spoke Chinese and Korean together. Listening in on snippets of their conversations, I tried to figure out if my suspicions were true.

They slept during the day and worked every night, always wearing strong fragrances and showy makeup and dresses. It wasn't hard to guess what my new job was to be.

"Please be seated."

When I entered the smoky office, the woman from the hill gestured to me to sit on a glossy leather sofa covered with a tiger skin. She was peering at me from behind a huge desk that made her small figure look somewhat absurd. I remained standing.

She got straight to the point. "So. What did you do over there?"

I stared at her. "I want to go back. You kidnapped me and shut me up here. I have a child I have to take care of—he's sick with a disease. As a woman, you must understand. Please, let me go."

Her close-set eyes squinted at me for a moment, and she nervously stubbed out her thin brown cigarette in the transparent ashtray on the desk. "I know nothing about it, and I don't care! I just heard about you from my brothers and bought you at a high price for my karaoke bar. We paid your friend on the hill. You saw it, too. Now you have to work to earn back what we paid for you."

That day, she wore spectacles with transparent purple lenses instead of sunglasses. Her eyebrows, which started from behind her glasses, were long lines shaped like two round mountains. It seemed that eyebrows were a big deal here.

She told me to call her *sajangnim* (boss) and took a sip of a tea from a transparent, round tea thermos. Inside the thermos purple flowers and green leaves danced languidly.

"Anyway, you're here; you'll work until you reimburse the price we paid for you, and then you can leave. Isn't this much better than a cave swarming with bugs? Think about it: you are an illegal vagrant in China. You are not supposed to set foot in this land, but you did. If someone reports you to the police, they'll come and drag you away within five minutes. We are protecting you. You don't know how dangerous it is outside. You can't imagine how runaways like you, especially women, usually end up." She cupped her chin in one hand and looked up at me. "You'll understand our kindness someday. The women working here all have good hearts; they'll be good friends for you. If something makes you uncomfortable, let me know. We'll do our best to take care of you."

She took another brown cigarette from a box. Her red and silver lighter spouted a thin flame, and she lit the cigarette with a long draw. "If you really want to get out of here, work hard. That's the fastest way. You can start after this weekend. I'll think over what role you can play best."

I got up to leave. "Remember, right now, you are a debtor," she said, gravely. "You can't leave before we're square. As long as you're here, your body belongs to me."

I wasn't Jia anymore, I was walking money.

The day after our arrival, I went outside with the deep-dimpled woman—I had learned her name was Mija—under the supervision of a man who haughtily informed us that he was going to turn us from country bumpkins into city women. The journey into town was my first glimpse of a Chinese city. The streets were so alive. The only thing I could compare it to was Pyongyang's World Youth Festival, though much noisier and more chaotic. I couldn't breathe very well because of the smoke. People and cars mixed together on the road; there were no traffic policemen. Vehicles moved wherever they wanted, and pedestrians rushed fearlessly in front of them, blocking the intersections. I was panic-stricken. The constant honking made me dizzy, and I couldn't see the sky above the rows of neon signs, big and small, mixing Korean and Chinese characters. Several giant signs featured widely smiling Korean women wearing *hanbok*.

"This place has everything," our warden said, beaming. "It has changed so fast. Look at those glittering signs—aren't they pretty? People who want to party come here to spend their money. That's where you come in. I hope you appreciate how lucky you are." He stroked Mija's hips and leered. Seeing this, I gripped her hand tightly and pulled her to my side. She looked at me in surprise and smiled.

Her revelations to me the night before had brought us closer. We both realized that it was in our interest to leave our misunderstandings behind and try to become friends.

The previous night, as I tried to fall asleep, Mija had tucked her arm under her head and lain down, facing me. I looked at her in the darkness with barely concealed contempt; I felt she had aided in my kidnapping.

"I have nothing left," she said.

The night air beyond the window was filled with laughter and music. Most of the women had gone, leaving behind only the noxious smell of cosmetics and perfume. I felt like vomiting.

"When I sent my baby down the river, my life floated away with her," Mija said, abjectly.

I turned onto my back and looked at the ceiling. It was much higher than in any of the other rooms I had seen so far. I thought of the cave, with its low ceiling and its stench, which I had learned to ignore after a while; perhaps we can get used to anything. I still felt hostile toward Mija. Truly, I cared more about Sangwon than about some wretch and her dead baby.

Mija turned onto her back as I had and went on. "I don't know why I said I would go with them." As she spoke, her voice grew louder, spreading into the whole room. "I felt so empty after I lost her. My baby's father was called my husband, but he never took care of us. He always flirted with other women. He told me he was starting his own business with another woman, and then they left, and never came back. I wonder if he even remembers our baby's name.

"I spent the days lost, with nothing to do. All I had to do was feed my baby, but we had nothing. Sometimes, my sister-in-law brought corn and rice, but eventually she stopped, and I couldn't blame her. She had three children of her own, and my brother didn't return from China for several months. My baby and I barely managed to live by eating cake flavored with pine bark. It eased the hunger, but it brought horrible physical pain. We were constipated; my baby was crying from pain all day and night. I even put soapy water into her anus with a rubber hose. I heard that some of my village people who couldn't go relieve themselves died because of it. I knew what the food did to us, but we ate it again and again. I couldn't stand my baby's screams. I decided to cross the river to save her."

Mija paused for a moment. I could hear her breathing heavily, trying to hold back her tears.

"I didn't know you were in the car until I got in," she said quietly. "When I asked them to take me, they told me to be at the mouth of the cave in three hours. When I saw you, I was surprised. They just said, 'She's not as smart as you are. We are trying to help her.' I didn't care about you, I even thought it would be better for me—at least I would see one familiar face when I got wherever they were taking me."

She turned away and sniveled quietly. I watched the ceiling in silence for a while and then slid into sleep.

Across the busy street, a hair salon was our destination. The hairdresser spoke Korean. She didn't ask me what I wanted; she just looked at me this way and that and then poured some chemicals onto my hair. My scalp burned, but when I tried to touch my head, she warned me, "You need this for your untamed hair."

While I suffered from whatever was in my hair, our warden teased me as though I was an animal in the zoo, and chatted gaily with his girlfriend on his cellular phone. He didn't leave my side for several hours. Occasionally, he threw some magazines onto my knee, saying, "You can kill time with those."

The magazines were colorful, showcasing many pretty women, but I couldn't concentrate. I looked out through the front door of the salon; so many people in the busy street. As darkness fell, the neon signs became brighter. Among them, one written in red letters caught my attention: Pyongyang Restaurant. It was a glowing three-story building, all glass. Women dressed in *hanbok* and men in bow ties seemed to flicker inside. All I could think of was how I could escape from this torture.

Several hours later, my hair had turned reddish-brown.

I didn't see the owner of the karaoke bar for days; it seemed she had completely forgotten about me. The women slept all day. At dawn, the smell of alcohol overpowered their cheap perfume; some women came back singing softly, while others came in frowning and swore themselves to sleep. Occasionally they would be riled up, and their loud laughter kept me up through the wee hours, until the men in the hall forced them to be quiet. When they woke up in the late afternoon, the women had returned to their reticent selves and quietly began preparations for another day at the karaoke bar.

When I first encountered the nightly routine, I was frightened by the drunken women. In the mornings they had hollow eyes and complained of headaches; at night their eyes were wild and out of focus. *That will be you soon*, someone seemed to whisper in my ear.

One evening, after most of the women had left for the evening, Mija and I cleaned up. We had opened the window completely to let some fresh air in when the owner came in and looked around the room.

Finding us, she commanded the eyebrowless woman, "Hey, help them make up."

"Will they start working tonight?" the woman asked, checking her curls in the mirror.

"Right. Hurry. It's time for the guests," the owner snapped.

"You should have said so before. I'm busy right now. And I'm not here to take care of novices."

"Stop whining. Since when are you busy? Nobody is interested in you, as usual."

The eyebrowless woman glared into her mirror for a moment, trying to find a word to spit back. Instead, she spun around to me. "Come here," she said without emotion.

Seeing the eyebrowless woman grab a cosmetic case, the boss departed. "Hurry," she said on her way out. "Make her hair smoother, too. The first impression is the most important—for her and for me."

The woman sneered, "That cross-eyed bitch is giving

up on me. She's getting worse." She took a strong-smell-ing lotion out of the case and rubbed it on my face. "This means you'll start a new life tonight." She watched my eyes for a moment and took out another bottle of lotion. "Just smile at the guests and serve them nicely. It's okay—after the first time, you'll think it's nothing."

"I'll think what's nothing? Are we singing and danc-ing for them? Or just serving food? Do we have to drink a lot?" Considering what I had seen, the job couldn't be that pleasant.

She didn't stop applying the lotion to my face. "You'll figure it out."

"I don't understand this place and the people here. I didn't risk my life for this," I complained.

Instantly, she lifted my face and powdered it from my forehead to my chin. Shutting my eyes to protect them from the powder, I heard her husky voice say, "Grow up and open your eyes. I'm satisfied with this life now. If you stop thinking about life, everything becomes simpler. When you open your eyes, a day starts. When you close your eyes, your day is over. What you eat and what you can buy will be the most important things to you sooner or later."

Having applied makeup to my face, the eyebrowless woman had me put on a shiny blue dress embroidered with silver, with holes that left my arms, my neck, chest, and thighs exposed. It felt like nothing more than a tiny towel, and my face grew hot. Once I was dressed, the owner took me to the first floor.

The lights in the hall were all on, and the building was alive. The owner stopped in front of a red door. "The better you serve the customers, the sooner you can get out of here and see your kid," she said, with menace in her voice.

She opened the door, and I saw a wall dominated by a giant TV screen surrounded by several smaller screens. Ruddy faces turned toward me. The room was filled with cigarette smoke. The smell of alcohol was in the air, and the music and the spinning lights were mesmerizing.

The owner pushed me into the room. "She's new."

I lowered my head instinctively, and a stout man rose to his feet and approached us. He rubbed the owner's back. "That's why I like you. How did you know we brought a really important guest tonight?" He leered at the owner, then at me.

"I read you better than your wife, right?" the owner said with a laugh. Patting the stout man's stomach, she said, "It's her first time here. She may not serve you so well, but look after her. Okay?" She wrapped her arm around my shoulder, overflowing with smiles as she spoke into my ear, but never taking her eyes off the others. "Do your best to serve these guests. They are my top customers." Her eyes glittered, but her mouth didn't smile.

All eyes seemed to be on me. I didn't raise my head or move a finger after the owner left. The gleaming lights were moving overhead as the stout man addressed his table, switching to Chinese from Korean. His voice was high and thin compared to his body.

Speaking into my ear, he said in Korean, "You'll have a good time here. We'll take such good care of you."

He sat me down on a sofa. The short dress made me uncomfortable, and I tried to cover my bare thighs, folding my arms in my lap. I counted seven pairs of legs under the table. Men and women's legs next to each other.

I wondered how Mija was doing. Earlier that evening,

a man had led her to the other side of the hall. The owner was displeased with Mija's very thin curly hairstyle, and had grabbed her hair and pulled it back behind her ears. Mija screamed in pain, but the owner just howled with laughter. "Do you think this is the nineteen seventies? How much will it cost to get the countryside out of you?"

The stout man handed me a cup of wine. "My Chinese friends want to know when you crossed the river."

I recoiled with fright to hear my secret mentioned so casually. *Does everyone know?* The fact that I had risked my life was mere entertainment to them. I didn't take the cup, keeping my eyes fixed on the ground.

The man wrapped his heavy arm around my shoulder and thrust the cup in front of my face. "I'm asking you when you came here."

A woman across from me answered in haste, "She just arrived. Like *sajangnim* said, this is her first night."

He said something in Chinese, pressing my forearm with his chubby hand. "You're brand new. Wasn't it cold crossing the river? Weren't you scared? The river must still be cold. This big guy will warm your body up—come here." He put his other hand on my thigh and tried to pull me toward him.

I pushed him back with all my might and jumped out off the sofa, shrieking, "Don't even think about touching one strand of my hair. I'm not joking. Do you understand?"

He landed on the woman sitting next to him. She cried out in pain.

"What the hell is this wench trying to do?" He stood up and tried to hit me.

The woman interjected, pulling him down. "Calm down. She's new, she's not yet been tamed by a man. Isn't she fresh, compared to us? You can train her gradually—it'll be fun. Come on! Sit down. Think about your Chinese guests. Didn't you say they would be good rich patrons? Consider your reputation. Come on!"

He stared fiercely at me for a moment and nodded his head to the other men several times, saying something in Chinese.

As he spoke, the woman walked over to me and put her face in mine. The smell of liquor engulfed me as she hissed, "Don't make trouble. Everything that you did will be reported. Be careful! You'd better listen to me, or I can't get my money either. Got it, moron?"

She turned back and smiled at the guests. Addressing them in Chinese, she said, "Let's play a game. You'll love it. You push the buttons on this remote control with your eyes closed, and you have to sing whichever song comes up. Let's go clockwise around the table, and no matter what song you get, you have to finish it. If one person can't sing his song, another person can volunteer, and then that volunteer can ask the person who couldn't sing to do whatever the volunteer orders. Drinking a glass of wine or a bottle of a beer, licking the sole of his foot, taking off a piece of clothing—anything. How about that?"

People clapped their hands in delight. The stout man roared with laughter. "This old fox knows every song here. And she likes to take guys' clothes off." He clapped his knees. "Okay. Let's do it! It's your turn to be naked, for once."

She smirked playfully, "Let's see! I'll go first."

As the other woman told me the rules of the game, I was stupefied. There was no way I could know any of the songs.

Seeing my reaction, the stout man smiled insidiously

and patted my knee. "There are North Korean songs, too. Don't worry. I'll sing for you if you don't know. I'll be your protector." He winked.

The woman who had suggested the game pushed several numbers, and words came up on the screen, accompanied by loud music. She grabbed a microphone with a broad grin, saying, "Oh, that's a hard one." She didn't make any mistakes in the rhythm or the lyrics, and the stout man danced and sang along with her. All the women passed the test. When a man couldn't sing, the woman in charge sang for him and ordered him to drink a big cup of wine. She asked a young man to take off his tie. "Let's start with the tie—we've got lots of time."

I was the last to sing. Before I could push the buttons, she handed me the microphone and whispered, "Keep your eyes slightly open and push one-thirty-five."

I was surprised; I didn't expect her to help me. Frantically, my fingers found the number 135, and the song that came out was the most popular one in North Korea at the time.

The stout man said loudly, "What a lucky night for you."

It was the song the other dancers and I had sung at the hotel for foreign customers on their last night in Pyongyang, and I was happy to sing it again. This time, I was singing for my survival, and a bolt of fire shot up my throat. I watched the woman who helped me. She was smoking a cigarette, listening without expression.

When I finished, she took the microphone and sniffed, "Huh. What did you do over there? Your voice sounds well trained."

The stout man stood up and clapped, holding a cigarette

in his mouth. "Okay. This time we'll go counterclockwise," he said, snatching the microphone back and handing it to me again.

The woman patted his stomach and said, "I'm the moderator of this game. I will take care of it. You, relax."

He snarled at her, "I'm the one paying the money. I will decide whatever I want to do."

She looked at him and shrugged. "As you wish..." Sitting down, she nodded to me to go ahead.

I stared at the man for a moment.

"What are you doing?" he demanded. "Push the buttons with your eyes closed, come on! Other people are waiting." He chortled, lighting a cigarette.

I pressed the buttons on the remote control randomly, trying to get a similar number. I thought the closest number would be another North Korean song. What popped up on the screen was in Chinese.

I turned to the others. "I can't sing this one. I don't know Chinese, it's not fair." I looked to the self-appointed moderator for support.

"A game is a game," she said. "Other people were punished, too. You should follow the rule." She leaned over the sofa.

"Come on. It's already started," the stout man said, pushing the microphone close to my mouth.

I stood there in silence, holding the microphone.

The woman in charge looked around the room. "Who wants to sing for her?"

No sooner had she asked than the stout man stripped me of the microphone and said, "This is my favorite song."

He sang it, throwing his bulk around. Other men and women joined him, and I watched them vacantly.

When the song was finished, he stroked his chin in mock thought. "What will I ask of you?" He walked around me several times, then stopped, as a slow grin spread across his face. "Take off your underpants."

Several men who understood Korean whistled and giggled.

I thought I had misheard it. Someone said, "What did that fat man say?"

"She has to start with an outer garment," the woman in charge said.

The stout man shook his head. "No, she wears a one-piece dress. I'm trying to be considerate, right?" He looked around at the others for their support. The Chinese men asked the others what he had said. Understanding, they smiled.

"Didn't you hear me? We're all waiting. Do it right now!" With his arms folded, he sat down on the sofa.

Shame rose from my stomach.

"Let's see what kind of underwear you people wear," he jeered.

"No. It's not going to happen," I said, glaring at him, flushing with anger.

He looked daggers at me. "You have enjoyed other people's punishment. You aren't exceptional. I am politely asking you to pay the penalty. 'When in Rome, do as the Romans do.' When you are in this room, do as the people in this room do." His glittering eyes frightened me. *"Right now!"*

I turned to leave, but he seized my arm, snarling, "I warned you. Don't embarrass me. They came here to enjoy themselves tonight, and if you leave like this, you will regret it, I promise."

I didn't know what I was doing; I only knew I had to

escape. When he dragged me back to the table, I grabbed the nearest object and slung it at his head. Shattered glass spread all over the room. With a sharp scream—"You wretch!"—he tumbled to the floor, clutching his head. There were shrieks as a few people lunged for me. I covered my head and crouched in a corner to make my body as small as possible.

At that moment, one thick, low, commanding Chinese voice emerged above the yelling. I didn't move. As he spoke, the others quieted. When I raised my head, the young man who had received the penalty of taking off his tie grasped the stout man by the arm and accompanied him out of the room.

The stout man's voice spread through the hall. "If you guys don't kill that crazy bitch, I'll burn this building down."
I was dragged to the room with the tiger-skin sofa, the *sajangnim's* office. Two men stood next to me, holding clubs covered in white towels. The boss opened the door with a bang and rushed into the room, her high heels clacking viciously. I raised my head and saw that her face had already turned a dark red.

Her eyebrows whirling, she bellowed, "You crazy vagrant! Do you know what you did tonight?" She kicked at my chest with her shoes. "You can never leave this place now. You're here for good."

She snatched a club from someone's hand and swung it around at me. I heard her snapping and snarling at me in time with the thuds on my body. I passed out.

When I opened my eyes, the woman who had helped me in the karaoke room was looking down at me, holding a cigarette. "They beat you the clever way," she said.

I tried to stand up, but my shoulders felt stuck to the floor like magnets.

"You'd better not move. They wrapped their clubs in towels—it prevents bruising. Your skin won't show any surface bruises, but you'll have a lot of them inside."

My nose felt clogged; it was hard to breathe. I looked around for a handkerchief and the woman gave me hers. It had a strong perfume smell. I unfolded it and blew my nose. There was a lump of blood. "Sorry," I rasped.

Her voice was flat. "It's okay. I have a bunch of hankies."

I looked at her cigarette. It was the first time I was ever tempted to smoke. "Thanks for trying to help me."

She moved her cigarette so the ashes would not drop on my face. "I wasn't helping you, I was trying to earn my money. That's our job, making them drink. They pay money and we satisfy their every dirty request. The more they drink, the better for our pockets, even though their behavior gets ugly. Don't think you're special, or purer than us!"

I broke in, "I have never thought I'm special, that's not why I made a fuss. I came to China for a better life, not for this. That doesn't mean I blame the women who work here."

She stood up and headed to the door, sighing, "I have to go," as she stepped into her orange high heels.

"Did you get your money for the night? Or did you get nothing, because of me?" I couldn't see her eyes, but I was sure she didn't like her job either.

"I got nothing. Thanks to you."

I felt ashamed of my behavior. "I'm sorry. I didn't mean for that to happen."

"Oh, well. I just hope I'm not in the same room as you next time." Stepping out of the room, she looked back. "Did you study singing?"

I nodded slightly.

"I liked your voice."

"Pack your things." The owner stalked into the room; I hadn't seen her since she had beat me senseless with a club. Mija was taking care of me. She had changed her hairstyle, and it looked so strange on her. My body had recovered somewhat, but I couldn't stop retching.

The owner found an empty, worn-out backpack in the corner of the room and threw it at me. "Hurry. Just pack the things you really need."

I could barely sit up. I stared at her. "I don't *have* anything to pack. How does a person who was dragged here against her will have time to bring her own things?"

Ignoring me, she snapped to two men at her side, "Take her."

"Where is she going?" Mija asked, fearfully.

The owner shouted, "Take her. Hurry!"

I tried not to move, but it was impossible to resist the men.

We were already near the end of the hall when the owner shouted behind me, "Your temper can destroy people around you. Leaving will be better for you and for us."

My feet never touched the ground; the men held me up by my armpits. I asked them, through gritted teeth, "Where are you sending me?"

"To a better place."

They dragged me to a white car in front of the building and forced me into the front seat. I screamed and struggled to free myself; I couldn't imagine a worse place, but I somehow knew that one was waiting for me.

I heard the sound of the car doors locking, and turned

to look out the back window at my captors as the car pulled away. The only difference between today and the day I was taken from the cave was the size of the car. It was a sedan, and it smelled like leather, not sour flesh. The car moved fast and without a sound.

I shot a sidelong glance at the driver. I could just make out his profile. It was the young man who had restrained the stout bully on my first night on the job.

16

Jin, Suspicious Guy

There were taxis everywhere. I remembered a director of the hotel back in Pyongyang proudly explaining to foreign guests that the city had over 100 taxis; I gave up counting after I reached 40. Pyongyang taxis were overpriced and definitely not popular with the natives, but the streets in China were filled with red taxis, and most had customers inside. Perhaps the taxis were not as expensive here.

The traffic was a stew of cars, bicycles, and pedestrians, all forging ahead without consideration for each other. I even saw two donkeys pulling a cart filled with straw and big black baskets. Watching through the window of the stranger's car, it seemed to me impossible that so many different kinds of transportation could flow in such a narrow space, without any control by traffic police.

Just a few minutes away from the karaoke bar, storefront

signs changed entirely to Chinese. It was the first time I felt I was in China. And I was sitting next to a strange Chinese man.

He drove in silence. I wanted to ask where he was taking me, but I was sure he spoke only Chinese. I remembered that he had been the calmest man in the room. A flurry of thoughts troubled my brain. *He was there with the stout man; he must be his friend. It's true he helped me escape, but he might take me to an even worse place. Why did he buy me? He might have bought me for the stout man. He'll take me to him and I'll be killed. Or he might be a policeman. He pretended to be a customer in order to look for North Koreans. His real purpose was to catch us. But the stout man made a fuss, so this man had to return to finish his mission. I had better run from this stranger.*

He sensed my restlessness and said something in Chinese. I was silent and gave him a sideways glance. A moment later, he asked me, very slowly, in English, "Do you speak English?" I nodded my head once, though I knew only a few words. He looked at me for a second, turned his eyes back to the steering wheel, and said, "Don't worry. I'm not heading to the police or taking you to the fat man."

He seemed to be reading my mind, and it made me more anxious.

He continued, "I know what kind of person you are. I know why you are so afraid, but I'm not someone who will denounce a woman."

I felt a rush of relief; he had saved me from the stout man, but what was he doing? What did he want from me?

"Did you buy me from them?" I asked suspiciously.

He looked straight ahead and nodded. "Yes."

I sat upright in the seat. "Why?" I fixed my eyes on the side of his face, gripping the door handle. If I didn't like his answer I would jump out of the car. Dying would be better than being dragged who knows where. I clenched my teeth.

After a long while, he replied, "Why? I don't know." He shrugged gently. "Have you met other North Koreans here?" he asked, changing the topic.

I didn't know what to make of him. His answers were unexpected and his questions were strange too. "Yes," I answered, shortly.

"How do they make a living here? Do they live as you do?"

I watched him, thinking about Sangwon and Mija. "Much worse."

"Jesus!" he sighed.

We drove for about an hour without speaking much. I asked him several times more what his real purpose was in buying me, to which he replied, "You just looked pathetic."

"I was in debt to the owner of the karaoke bar," I said. "Your sympathy saved me from repaying that, I guess." I didn't know what else to say. Instead of feeling grateful, fear of being in a car with a strange man rose up inside me. "What will you do with me?"

"I don't know. I haven't thought about that. I was just busy negotiating the price with your boss," he answered, as though it was the most natural thing in the world.

"How much did you pay? I'll pay you back. I am not a dog waiting for a master to come along." My voice reflected my embarrassment.

He spoke lightly, "First of all, I don't raise dogs, I'm too busy to take care of dogs. Anyway, you were more expensive than the other women, according to the owner of that karaoke bar. But how would you pay me back? Did you bring money from your country?"

I couldn't reply. Of course he knew I didn't have any money. I felt I was pushed against the wall. Did he buy me out of sympathy? He must have something to hide. I was busy trying to read his mind, and he seemed preoccupied with trying to read mine.

"I don't know much about North Korea," he continued, "but I know people there don't have contact with foreigners and foreign things. I have a hunch that you, however, may not be typical, that you had some sort of high position. Am I right?" he cast me a searching glance.

I remained silent and looked ahead, avoiding his eyes.

"It's okay. It doesn't matter.... You don't have to tell me if you don't want to." We rode in silence for a moment. At length, he said, "When I saw you in that awful place, I just felt you really wanted out. And this was what I could do."

We rapidly left the city behind; buildings became fewer and fewer, replaced by tree-covered mountains. The western sky lit up with the crimson glow of the setting sun and I felt for the first time that China was beautiful. After passing several big houses, he stopped the car in front of a fancy one, and got out of the car to smoke. Watching the sunset, he stretched his body. He was much taller than other men I had met.

I didn't move from my seat. We were all alone; I felt it wouldn't be so hard to escape. Should I run away? Could I run away? If I did, where would I go next? I looked around the car. Behind the back seat, the head of a small bulldog doll bobbed back and forth.

When I turned back, the man was looking at me with a half smile. "Are you going to stay there all night?" He leaned in through the driver's side window. "This is my house."

He walked around the car and opened the door for me. I

got out, and he locked it, saying, "Let's go." I didn't budge
an inch. "No one will hurt you. It'll be okay." He held my
arm lightly and led me into the house. At that moment, my
gut told me he was someone who wouldn't lie to me. I followed him inside.

The house was dark and seemed empty; the entryway was
bare and chilly compared to the warm air outside.

"It will be a little bit cold, sorry; I haven't used this house
for a while. I'm doing my best to make it cozy, though."
He looked for the light and turned it on, and I caught the
smell of new furniture. "Like you, I've just arrived. I don't
know this place very well, either, but I like the surroundings. There are not a lot of neighbors—I haven't talked to
any yet, but a couple seemed nice."

In the living room, he drew aside ivory curtains to re-
veal almost an entire wall made of glass. I could see a few
houses and a thickly wooded hill. "Isn't it pretty?" my host
said. "It's hard to find a house with this kind of view in
China." With a satisfied smile, he took in the scene for a
moment, then stroked a cream-colored sofa, which looked
soft. "Let me introduce you to the house. Come on." After
several steps, he wheeled around and said, "Oh, we'd better
eat something first. Right? I haven't eaten since noon."

He took off his jacket and hung it on the back of the sofa,
motioning me to follow him. Opposite the big window
was a kitchen with stainless-steel cupboards and appliances.
He opened a huge, fully stocked refrigerator and took out
several plastic bags containing meat and vegetables.

"You don't have to cook today, because it's your first day
here. But you should cook for yourself starting tomorrow. I
don't have time to cook for you every day."

I had one foot inside the kitchen and one out, and I stayed that way while he cooked. He didn't ask me to sit down or help him. He was engrossed in his task; he was really good at it, too. He took a large, square knife from a drawer, and made a racket chopping the vegetables into tiny pieces at lightning speed. He prepared a vegetable and chicken dish with rice, too much for two people to eat.

"I know Koreans don't like oily food, so I bought some spicy sauce for you. But I don't know how much you want to use. I'll put it here, separately, so you can use as much as you like."

He flew around the kitchen. The faster he cooked, the faster he spoke. Finally, clapping his hands twice, he turned back to me.

"Okay, I think I'm pretty much done. Let's eat."

He gave me an empty dish, chopsticks, and a spoon. When I caught a whiff of the dish, I was suddenly famished.

"Big spoons, right? Isn't that Korean style?" He handed me a large, flat spoon. It seemed new. "I'm half Korean too, actually."

My head snapped toward him, and he shrugged slightly. "My father was Korean. I don't talk about it unless people ask. I'm kind of ashamed that I can't speak any Korean. My father was too lazy to teach me, or too busy. If I had grown up here, I would have learned it from other Korean-Chinese people."

He sat down at the kitchen table. Holding chopsticks in one hand, he looked up at me, still standing. "What are you doing? You're not going to eat? Come on, have a seat."

He ate without another word. I had eaten almost nothing at the karaoke bar, and hunger was storming up in my stomach. The food was a bit oily, but the flavor only sparked my appetite further. We ate in silence. Longing for that kind of regular meal was changing the destinies of so many people in North Korea.

When he put his chopsticks down on the table, I stopped eating. I stood up with my plate and reached for the other dishes, but he took them from my hands.

"I will take care of everything tonight. You can do it starting tomorrow."

I stepped away from him, and he put the dishes in the sink, throwing some leftovers in the trash can next to it. I thought about the *kkotjebi,* begging for food all day. That trash would be dinner for several *kkotjebi.* He scrubbed the plates and utensils and returned them to the cupboard. Inside the cupboard were too many bowls and plates for one person.

"I haven't tried North Korean food before. Oh, but I like *bibimbab* and *naengmyeon,* or whatever you call that cold noodle dish. If you know how to make them, would you, sometime?"

I didn't answer. So long as I didn't know what he really wanted from me, I knew I couldn't feel secure. My head was spinning. *I should be ready to bolt, just in case. That's the lesson I've learned in my life. Why did he buy me? Does he want me to be his sex slave, like the other men? Is that why he brought me here, to this isolated place?* My fear returned with a rush.

Staring at his back, I said, "I was in that hell against my will. Don't be confused and think you can do whatever you want just because you bought me."

He continued washing the pans in silence for a moment, then said quietly, "You'd better learn Chinese. I know it's hard to learn a foreign language as an adult. But if you can't speak Chinese, you'll live in fear of being arrested. You speak English, but it's not perfect either. If you meet Chinese people, you can tell them in English that you are from South Korea. But if you run into South Koreans, they'll know. Living here without speaking Chinese isn't difficult—you can go to the Korean-Chinese districts if you need something. But you are in China now. Learning Chinese will be better for you."

I replied, as if he had not spoken, "You don't have to pretend you are a nice guy. I know every man wants one thing. I'll kill myself if you try to force yourself on me, but I'll kill you first, I'm warning you."

He dropped the pan in the sink with a clatter. Swinging around, he glared at me, his face twitching. "You know what? I am not starving for sex. If I really wanted it, I would have taken it already. Finding women here is not at all difficult, and you are not as attractive as you think."

He left the kitchen, and I stood holding on to the chair with one hand.

"Come here," he called from the next room. "I'll show you around the house."

He pointed to the bathroom and then took me to a room on the second floor. "This is your room. These are some clothes you can wear—I didn't know your size. If they are too big or too small, let me know. I can return them and exchange them for the right sizes." He continued, "The second floor is all yours. I'll use the first floor. Take a rest tonight. If you have any question, you can call me. Good night." He started down the stairs.

"Why are you helping me like this? I know nothing is free, and I really need to know what you want from me."

He looked at me, frustrated. "I don't want anything from

you. If you want to run away, you can. I just wanted to help you. But, whatever you do, stay away from the police. First of all, think about how you can survive here. I didn't promise I could help you forever—you'll have to find a way to stand on your own feet. Good night." He closed the door.

I watched the door for a while. Everything had happened so fast; I had been in hell only hours ago. I locked the door and pushed the bed in front of it, so he couldn't get in. I lay down with my head next to the door, so as to hear the slightest sound on the other side. As soon as my body hit the bed, I realized how tired I was.

I didn't want to think anymore; it didn't get me anywhere. Tomorrow, I would ask one more time what he really wanted from me. My mind still swirling, I fell asleep.

The morning sun flooded in through a window. When I opened my eyes, I realized I hadn't even changed my clothes, or covered myself with a blanket. My body no longer ached. Getting up, I opened the door slightly and stole a peek down the hall. It was perfectly quiet. The shadows of trees played on the floor and wall opposite a window. He seemed to have left already.

I found a message fastened to the door:

> Dear Miss X,
>
> Just now I realized I don't even know your name. I hope you will tell me later. I had to leave—I will probably be back late tonight. You can have a rest. There is food in the kitchen and some books that I bought for you to study Chinese. They are all written in Korean. Have a look at them.

I'll talk to you later. Have a good rest. Oh, by the way, I don't recommend that you go outside. We can walk around together when I return.

I hope you have a restful day.

Sincerely,

Jin (金)

P.S. My name is Jin Xuezhen, in Chinese, which is Kim Hakjin in Korean.

He had the most common Korean surname—his father must be Korean, so perhaps he wasn't lying.

I shut the door and looked around the room more closely. Like the rest of the house, it smelled of new furniture, and everything was white, ivory, or transparent. I found some Chinese textbooks and tapes on the desk. I might as well study this strange language, I thought. When I opened the ivory closet next to the desk, I discovered clothing hanging inside. I checked the clothes piece by piece, until I got to a pair of blue jeans. I had always wanted to try on jeans, but it was impossible at home; the government didn't allow them because they are symbols of the West and not suited to "feminine modesty." One of my coworkers always sighed with envy when we had the chance to watch Western television programs for language classes. She'd say, "I want to try on those tight blue pants, too. Don't you think they look nice?"

Thinking of her, I smiled to myself. I took the jeans and a white shirt off their hangers. Closing the closet, I went to a corner of the room and hid behind a chair; I was scared out of habit. The jeans weren't as tight as I had seen on TV, but they fit, and I felt comfortable in them.

I went downstairs, scouring the house for people. On

my tour of the house the night before, my nerves had kept me from paying attention. It was hard to believe all that space was for just one person. I wondered what kind of job could maintain such a fancy house. In the living room, he had covered two entire walls with many kinds of small cars on ledges. A huge TV stood against the third wall—it was about as big as the one in the reception hall of the hotel where I had worked in Pyongyang.

There were several photographs along the hall to his room. I inspected them carefully, as though looking at a person's entire history. Jin's thick eyebrows were hereditary. One picture showed him with his parents. I couldn't tell that his father was Korean and his mother Chinese; I just saw them as people, like me. It became clear why he had such dark skin; most of the pictures were taken at the beach. In several of them he was with foreigners, a big smile on his face.

I realized I didn't have that kind of record of my life. I had no pictures with my grandparents or my sister, and their figures were vanishing from memory. All my pictures were taken during dance performances, when I was in thick makeup and wore a feigned smile. I had burned them all before coming to China.

There was a photo of a woman with a wide smile, her arms wrapped around Jin's neck from behind; they looked happy. She might be his girlfriend or wife, I thought, and if he had wanted to seduce me, he would have taken that picture down.

I went back to the sun-filled living room. The sunshine tempted me sorely, and I decided to leave the house. If the door was locked, it would mean he wanted to shut me up in the house, and I would have to run away. Nervously, I gripped the doorknob. It twisted open smoothly.

Right, I thought. Maybe he really doesn't care. It's possible. A rich person might help a desperate woman out of fleeting sympathy, like buying a dog on the street. I felt so sad; I was becoming distrustful of everyone.

I stepped outside and looked up at the sky, letting my face bask in the sun. From the outside, the house looked like a simple two-story brick edifice. I walked around for a while. To the left was a wide green field dotted with ponds. The houses could be counted on two hands. I walked toward the ponds. A few people appeared in the distance, and I scrambled back to the house, seized with fear.

Inside, I felt much safer; I was still afraid of the outside. I took a shower, scrubbing hard to get rid of the dirt my life had collected. I wished all my pain would disappear down the drain, but I couldn't get rid of Sangwon. He might still be looking for me. He didn't mention the exact name of the place where we had stayed in the cave, but I vaguely remembered it being in the Baekdu Mountains. I thought about Kangmin and his friend, Bangmu. What did they tell Sangwon? He's smart; he must have seen through their lies.

I thought about Gun and Sun, too. They might be close by, perhaps they passed through that same cave, took the same steps. I understood now why Gun was so worried about Sun being in China alone. Who knows, maybe Gun had already found her and they were together: that was what I hoped for most.

After showering, I fell into the most comfortable sleep I had had since arriving in China.

When I woke, it was dark again, and completely quiet. I

went downstairs, but there was no sign of Jin. Feeling hungry, I searched the refrigerator, settling on some rice and vegetables.

As I was preparing my dinner, I heard Jin clear his throat behind me. I whirled around, holding a sharp knife.

He smiled and said, "Go ahead and eat. Actually, I haven't eaten either. If you don't mind, could you make enough for me?" Sitting down, he said, "How was your day? Did you rest enough?"

I continued chopping. "Yes, I slept all day."

"That's great. You must have gotten over your fatigue. Do you want me to cook?" He rolled up his sleeves.

"No, I'm almost done." I hurriedly put the food into some small dishes and served them. Jin smacked his lips.

We sat together and ate. "How are the clothes?" Jin asked, eating with gusto. "Do they fit?"

I was too flustered to answer his questions, and I didn't raise my head. I depended on him now.

I noticed that Jin held his rice bowl in his hand, moving it to his mouth to eat. My grandfather always instructed me not to hold my rice bowl in my hand. He would say, "Only *ssangnom*"—the lowest class in dynastic times—"eat like that. Don't even think about picking up your rice bowl. The spoon is for rice. Chopsticks are for dishes. Don't lower your head. Raise your head while you are eating."

Jin didn't use his spoon at all; he preferred chopsticks for tossing lumps of steamed rice into his mouth. He seemed like a starving child, eating everything up before someone could take his meal away, and I smiled at the sight. Seeing me, he stopped suddenly and asked with his mouth full, "What? Is something wrong?"

I quickly looked down at the table. "No." I put a load of

vegetables in my mouth to show him I didn't want to talk anymore.

"I'm glad you've started smiling." He put the empty rice bowl down on the table. "Starting tomorrow, a girl will come to see you every day. She's Korean-Chinese, and will teach you Chinese. She's the only one who knows you're here, so you'll be safe with her. Whenever you have questions or problems, ask her, because I won't be here much."

I stopped eating and said, "Thank you for doing all of this."

He lowered his chopsticks. "Are you not going to ask again why I am helping you?" His skin was as dark as Gun's, but smoother, as if covered with wax.

"It's sometimes hard to explain why people do what they do," Jin went on. "I can't tell you in one or two sentences why I helped you. When I first saw you, I just felt that you shouldn't be treated like that. I felt as if I had committed a sin. Actually, before moving here I'd heard stories from a South Korean friend about North Korean defectors and how badly they were treated. I hadn't paid that much attention to those stories at all. But when I saw you, I was shocked; I didn't actually believe this was happening here. I'm not a philanthropist, only a businessman, focused on making money. Just consider yourself lucky. I don't know what the next steps will be. I don't know where you'll want to go, but I will try to help you as much as possible."

What could I say to that? He wasn't like the other Chinese—not like the stout man in the bar or the karaoke owner.

"Do all Chinese people speak English, like you?" I asked, surprising myself.

He looked at me, amused. "Is that what you wanted to

ask me?" he laughed. "No. Actually, I grew up in England, and I just returned to China. That's why this house looks so new. The people in the karaoke bar wanted to do business with me—they were trying to impress me." Jin studied my facial expression. "But it was the worst place I have ever been in."

I carried our dishes to the sink. "I'm sorry I was so aggressive yesterday," I said.

"No. If I were in your situation, I would behave worse. Don't worry about that—I've already forgotten."

He wiped the table with a small white towel. "By the way, is there anything else you need?"

Returning the dishes to the cupboard, I said, "No. I'm really fine now."

"If you have something that you are reluctant to ask me, you can discuss it with the girl who will come tomorrow. Don't hesitate."

I sat down in front of him. "Would you do something for me, later, when you have time?"

"What is it?" he asked.

"I want to go outside." I wanted to see everything—see where I was, with my own eyes.

"Okay. The day after tomorrow, I'll be off, and we'll go outside. Or did you mean right now?" He rose to his feet and picked up his jacket from the chair.

"Right now?" I asked, gazing up at him from my seat.

"Yes. Why not? Let's go—maybe just for a short time."

His car moved smoothly through the countryside, with the windows half-open. The fresh night air clouded as the numbers of neon lights increased.

As we entered the city, Jin said, "There are several busy

districts here, they're the young people's favorites."

We passed a big statue of Mao Zedong, the Great Leader of China, holding up his right hand. His pose was identical to that of Kim Il Sung at Mansudae in downtown Pyongyang. Lights surrounded him, illuminating his face. All about the statue were packs of people and the sounds of music.

"That's the largest and most famous square here," Jin said. "All kinds of people gather here at night. The young girls and boys dance to new music, and old people enjoy themselves with traditional dances. Let's come here next time—it's really interesting. You can understand the changes inside China watching all the generations together. You know, China was like your country; it had the same ideology, but that all changed so quickly after Mao Zedong passed away. So many changes... I thought North Korea would take a similar path after your Mao passed away."

I glanced at the square. Groups of people sat right below the statue, their radios on the ground next to them. How did they dare sit there, so close? They seemed so relaxed, joyful. I could see their teeth when they smiled.

Jin drove us to a district glittering with lights. Smiling people were everywhere, and laughter filled the air. At first, I dared not watch people's faces through the window of the car.

"It's okay," Jin said. "Nobody will recognize you; you're just like everyone else on this street."

He took me to an ice-cream shop whose high ceiling was filled with colorful balloons. The people working inside wore bright uniforms and hats, and the customers chatted noisily, laughing and holding their treats. There were even old people.

"I like to eat ice cream after a meal," Jin said. "At times, I really miss the sweet things I had in England. Ice cream is easy to find anywhere here—Chinese people love it. Even in freezing weather, you'll see people holding ice cream with their thick gloves. You want to try it?"

He led me to the counter. There were so many square boxes underneath the glass. "Are they all different flavors of ice cream?" I asked in disbelief.

"Yes! Choose two of them."

In the end, I deliberated for too long and Jin chose for me. Leaving the shop with our ice creams, I felt the wind brush against my face. Feeling ice cream softly melting in my mouth, I looked up at the sky. There were no stars, not even one.

"Can we walk a little bit?" I asked him, looking at the hazy sky.

"Yes, sure. Let's go to this way."

I strolled happily along, sometimes bumping into other people gently as I went. I looked at them in panic, but they didn't care. Nobody cared about me, nobody watched me. I walked and walked, trying to remember everything I saw.

During our second lesson together, I asked my Chinese teacher, Hyunmi, how to get to the Korean-Chinese area from Jin's house. She told me it was easy to run into *kkotjebi* on the streets near the Korean-Chinese center.

"They block people walking on the street and reach out for gifts," Hyunmi said. "They also congregate around the Korean and Korean-Chinese churches nearby. I always see the same kids after worship on Sunday. Some of my friends are really close to them and always give them money. They call to us, 'Sisters, brothers, we are all Koreans.' These words always stop me in my tracks. I hear they sleep to-gether in a private video-viewing room at night. They look so pathetic. None of them has a child's face anymore."

I made up my mind to go see them, hoping to find Sangwon. I would ask the children whether they had seen a small boy with a limp. I just couldn't be happy living on my own like that; I was deeply worried about him. And I knew he was searching just as hard for me.

One day, some two weeks after arriving at Jin's house, I woke up early and waited for Jin to leave the house. He ate a simple breakfast—two fried eggs and fruit with tea—and departed quickly for his company. I wondered how he'd have energy for the morning with no rice on his plate. He was never comfortable when I woke up early to cook for him, so I would wait in my room until he'd left.

As soon as I heard his car, I called Hyunmi and said I needed to postpone our Chinese study session to the next day because I wasn't feeling well. Stuffing some paper mon-ey and coins in my pocket, I left the house.

The bus slowed as it approached the bus stop but didn't stop completely. A dark-skinned woman stuck her head out of the window next to the door. Opening the door, she pulled me forcefully by my shirt and lifted me into the bus. I looked at her with surprise, but she didn't meet my eyes; she just stuck out her open palm. Holding on to the back of a seat, swaying all about, I managed to put a one-yuan coin in her hand; it appeared unnaturally bright against her skin.

The instant I saw Korean words mixed with Chinese on the signs of the stores, I jumped off the bus, which barely slowed down. From the street, I watched it stir up dust as it bounced away into the distance.

I looked around the bus stop so I would know how to

get back. There was a giant poster with the yin–yang symbol, advertising Korean Airlines. Across from it was a gray building adorned by a cardboard Korean woman in a *hanbok*, bowing politely. Finding a wide intersection, I crossed and proceeded straight ahead.

The weather was hot; the wind, thick with dust, felt like cobwebs clogging my throat. I regretted wearing the jeans, as they stuck to my legs. Women rode bicycles in short skirts and men pulled their shirts up to their chests, showing their bare stomachs. I felt embarrassed by them and averted my eyes. Old men waved fans, sitting in the shadows beneath the buildings. I decided to buy the first fan I saw.

As I walked, I looked everywhere for *kkotjebi*. I saw people sitting down along the crowded streets, mats and paper spread in front of them. The fortune-tellers' signs bore the yin–yang symbol with a person's face in the center. Fortune-tellers sat on each block at about ten-meter intervals. I saw a customer with a serious face, sitting in front of an old man and listening ardently to his predictions.

I couldn't find a single *kkotjebi* on the street. It was growing hotter and more humid, and my body was tiring out. Did I get off at the wrong bus stop? No, I checked several times. A lot of people on the street spoke Korean, but I hadn't found a church yet. I resolved to go further.

As I was waiting for the light to change, someone gripped my arm tightly from behind. I was startled but turned nimbly to find a man smiling at me. It was one of the men from the karaoke bar.

"Hey, what are you doing here?" he said with a grin. I pretended not to know him and tried to wrest free of his hand. His grip tightened. "Hey, can't you even say hi to me? Come on! Don't pretend you don't know me. I've been thinking about you. How have you been?"

He didn't let go of my arm, but whistled admiringly. "Oh, you don't look like a beggar anymore. Is the guy who bought you good to you? Look at you! Money is the fastest way to change people, isn't it?"

I stared at him with annoyance. "Let me go." People were stepping around us to cross the road.

I tried to wriggle free, but he locked his arm in mine and said, "Let's go someplace for a cup of coffee. I wanted to be friends, we just didn't have time. But now look! Don't you think this is fate? Let's go, we'll have some fun after coffee." He winked.

I pushed him away and stomped on his foot. He screamed and swore, "Fuck, this bitch—" I tried to leap away, but the signal had changed to red, and I had no choice but to jump into traffic.

Chasing after me, he shouted, in Korean, "She's a North Korean runaway! She took my money! Catch her!" Then he shouted something in Chinese. All at once, people's eyes fixed on me, and within seconds, men in uniforms were rushing after me.

I tried to run but bumped into people at every turn. One of the policemen caught me by my hair. He pulled me up to him, and another policeman grabbed my waist. Bystanders formed a circle around us. When I looked back, the man from the karaoke bar was standing in the distance, watching me. Catching my eye, he waved, smiled, and walked away.

I was dragged away by three men, two holding my hands and one pushing my head down hard. I felt pain in my shoulders, but I couldn't scream. I was taken to a small police station and thrown into an empty prison cell. They called over a young, pink-faced man with pimples who was sitting at a table reading a magazine. He looked at me and asked, in Korean, "Are you North Korean?"

I was silent. He held out his hand. "If you are not, prove it. Give me your ID."

I replied in English, "I want to make a phone call."

"I asked you to give me your ID," he said, in Korean.

I stood up before him and said, "I want to make one call. Someone will come. Until then, I won't do anything." I felt it was best not to speak. I had to contact Jin. I crouched down in the corner of the cell and repeated to myself, "I'm not going back there. I'm not going back there."

He looked at me and inclined his head, then went back to confer with the others. I could understand a bit of what they said—they were debating whether I was really North Korean. They picked up the phone to call someone.

Several minutes later, a female police officer breezed into the cell. She stood me up and investigated my whole body, finding only some Chinese cash—no ID, not even a scrap of paper. I spoke to them in English again and gestured, "Please. I want to make one call. One call."

After discussing it among themselves, they handed me a phone, and through the bars of the cell I stuck out my index finger to dial Jin's number. I'll never forget the endless minute I stood and listened to the number ringing. Jin was never home in the middle of the day, but it was the only telephone number I had. Given another chance, I would call Hyunmi.

After several rings, the sound suddenly cut off.

"*Wei?*"

Through the thin line of the telephone, Jin's low voice

shot into my ear. I couldn't respond at first, I didn't know how to explain where I was.

"Hello. Is it Jia?" After a silence, he repeated the question. "Jia, is it you?"

"Jin, please help me."

"Jesus Christ, Jia! Where are you?" he shouted.

I explained what I could, that I was in the hands of the police, at a station near the Korean-Chinese center.

"Okay. I'll be there soon. Don't say *anything,* okay? I'll be right there."

I hung up, they took the phone back, and the man who spoke Korean made a phone call. In Korean, I heard him say, "Right, you guys come here and check her out." Catching my eyes as they filled with confusion, he spoke to the others in Chinese. Parts of what he said I could understand: "I called them. They'll come...and figure out whether she's theirs or not." He went back to his desk and opened the magazine he had been reading.

I was stunned. He must have called the embassy or some agents from North Korea. I stared at the door; if they got there earlier than Jin, there was no hope. I tried to stay calm and not watch the door, but I couldn't control my shaking hands.

I shut my eyes tight, regretting my decision to come to the Korean-Chinese district by myself. Why didn't I tell Jin first?

At that moment, someone banged on the iron bars of the cell, causing an uproar.

"Jia! Hey! It's me!" It was Jin, puffing hard in front of me.

I leaped up and grabbed the bars. I could barely open my mouth, but I managed to whisper, "Please, Jin, get me out of here."

Only the thickness of the bars separated us. He lowered his voice and said, "What are you doing here? Why are you here?"

He rebuked me. I couldn't control myself and started sniffling. "I didn't know this would happen. I'm sorry."

Through the bars, I clutched at his jacket and pleaded with him. "North Korean investigators are coming. I have to leave before they get here, please."

He headed to the policemen and bowed to them. They talked for a while and Jin patted one man's shoulder, smiling, nodding his head on and on. My heart beat loudly, and my eyes returned frantically to the door.

Jin came back with a man wielding a ring of rusty keys. The man searched through them slowly, looking for the right one. I wanted to snatch the keys out of his hands and open the cell door myself.

Standing behind him, Jin said, "Once you're out, get right in the car, okay? Stay inside, okay?" He stressed each syllable. I could feel his nervousness as well.

Finally I heard the sound of the key turning smoothly. As soon as the policeman opened the door, I jumped out and followed Jin. His car was right in front of the police station, and I rushed in as he ran back into the station in a flurry. I sighed and leaned back in the seat.

At that moment, three men strode brashly into the police station. I couldn't see their faces very well, but I sensed they must have been the agents the Chinese police had called, and I sank into my seat. Jin came out with flushed cheeks and ran to the car, finding me crouched under the dashboard. Jumping in, he cranked the engine and we sped away.

"Is everything okay?" I asked as I straightened up in the seat.

"It's okay, let's just get out of here."

We turned onto a wider road and right into a traffic jam.

"As you feared, those were the North Koreans. I was just finishing with the policemen when they came in, so I tried to get out quickly." Holding the wheel, he loosened his necktie. His face was dripping with sweat.

"Why did they let me go?" I asked.

He glanced at me. "I told them you are my *ernai*. That means my lover. I said I bought you and lost sight of you while we were shopping. They said that when they catch you next time, they'll send you back right away and arrest me, too."

I listened in silence; the excuse didn't matter. *I don't have to go back!* Those words spun around my brain. I was sure he must have had to strike a deal with the police.

"And then?" I looked at him.

He whistled shortly and smiled. "Don't worry. Everything is okay. I showed my appreciation to them."

Jin's deep voice pounded through the car. "Why did you go there by yourself? Why didn't you tell Hyunmi or me? She called me and said you were sick, so I went to the house to check on you. When I found you were gone, I knew something was wrong. If I hadn't gone back, or picked up the phone, what would you have done?"

He paused, collecting himself. "Whenever you want to go into town, we'll take you to the Korean-Chinese neighborhoods. But for the time being, it's not safe for you to go by yourself."

I wanted to crawl into a mouse hole. I was trouble to Jin, worse than a pet. I sulked. "I just wanted to find my friend," I said meekly.

He shook his head and stepped on the accelerator. "Oh, Jia, are you out of your mind? You have to take care of yourself first."

The cars were thinning out. Feeling the air conditioner in the car and watching the scenery go by, I couldn't believe it was stifling outside. Everything looked so peaceful. The trees looked even fatter than the day I arrived at Jin's house.

To come so close to losing all this made me shiver with fright.

We passed several small stores and houses, and came upon a crowd of people surrounding some police cars blocking the road.

"What's going on here?" Jin said, honking the horn. After a moment, he gave up and said, "Let's see what's happening." He pulled over and we walked toward the center of the crowd. I saw five women seated on the ground, weeping. Some women were hugging men; one woman grabbed on to a policeman's leg. Clicking their tongues and shaking their heads, spectators watched the scene. Some muttered in Korean, "Tsk. That's too much."

There was an old man next to me, with three deep wrinkles in his forehead. "What's going on?" I asked him.

He glanced at me and explained, "The policemen rounded those women up just now. They're all from North Korea and are married to Korean-Chinese men. The policemen are trying to take them back to North Korea, but they don't want to leave. That's why they are crying and begging."

One woman, pregnant and in tears, nodded to a policeman. The policeman told her husband in Korean that a superior office had given the order and nothing could be done. Other officers smoked at a distance and watched the scene, barely interested.

The old man said, "If their husbands have money, it'll be fine. There are a lot of North Korean women married to Korean-Chinese men in this village. But those husbands can't pay the fines—they spent all their money buying their wives."

Having seen enough, the old man turned to go, talking to himself. "They are not harmful. Why not let them live here?"

The policemen dragged the women away as their husbands looked on, helpless. The pregnant woman's husband mourned bitterly, slapping the ground.

Jin grabbed my arm and tugged. "Let's go. This place isn't safe for you either." We got in the car, but I couldn't turn my eyes away.

"The director of the police station said that investigators are getting stricter," Jin said, watching the police cars speeding in the opposite direction. "It really looks like he wasn't kidding."

The rest of the ride was silent. When we arrived back at the house, I was overcome with fatigue. I collapsed on the bed and fell asleep.

That day brought several changes to our life, Jin's and mine. I asked Hyunmi to teach me Chinese one more hour each day, and I spent hours watching Chinese TV. I practiced my Chinese with Jin daily, despite my embarrassment. He developed a new habit of collecting newspaper clippings related to North Koreans in China.

One morning, in the middle of breakfast, Jin said, "There must be some way to solve your problem. Let's try to see what we can do."

But when he returned that evening, he seemed depressed at the sight of me. "Damn it, I can't understand it. Since when did we start following international law so carefully!"

I couldn't get legal status in China, and Jin tried to explain why, but I couldn't understand much of what he said. One night, he brought home a thick book about international law, written in English, and we stayed up all night reading it. He murmured, "It seems that there is still no legal process for getting status for you here."

"Whether we are defectors or refugees is important?"

"Yes, because it determines whether you'll have protected status."

He threw the book on the sofa.

"Unless you're in a country that admits you legally…" I couldn't hear his voice well.

"What did you say?"

"The South Korean government protects North Korean refugees and lets them live there as citizens."

He told me stories he'd read in the media of people who had defected from North Korea, and how they'd arrived at their final destinations.

"It could be dangerous," Jin mused, "but it would be worth it."

I sipped tea quietly. "Jin, I won't leave this place."

"What do you mean?" He peered at me.

"I can't leave this place."

Jin's eyes were wide. "Why not? If you can get to another country safely, you'll be protected."

"Jin, how do we know other countries will welcome me? If they don't accept me, where do I go next?" Before Jin could answer, I continued, "I owe so much to people I left there. My official defection could endanger their lives."

I had talked about my secret life, my family and people I had met. I had even mentioned Seunggyu; he could be in danger as the ex-boyfriend of a national traitor. It wasn't his fault that he fell for me. Then I told Jin Sangwon's story.

"I don't know whether my family is alive or not, but I can't gamble their lives for my own sake. They've already risked their necks for me. I can't ignore the people who stood behind me." I thought about Director Park, Teacher Song, and the director of the orphanage.

Jin's eyes faded with disappointment, and I forced some cheer into my voice. "Jin. I need to try to survive here first. I think it's too early to give up on this place. My situation is much better than others like me, and I'm grateful for that. Here I still have hope that I'll hear from my friends."

"Okay, Jia. I understand. Let's try to find a way for you to settle here safely and not be afraid of being dragged back," Jin said, all smiles again, showing his orderly white teeth.

One afternoon, several weeks later, Jin threw open the door and blew into the living room. "Jia, where are you?" he cried.

I was with Hyunmi, studying Chinese, as usual. After two hours of study, my brain had given up. I envied the Korean-Chinese, like Hyunmi, who could speak both languages fluently. We were about to drink green tea when Jin's voice startled us. Out of breath, he looked at us in turn and sank down wearily into the sofa, but a confident smile lingered on his face.

"I'm making tea right now. You'd better drink something first." I turned to go back into the kitchen.

"No. Come here. Sit here first. I have something to tell you." He was still panting.

I sat down on the sofa. "What's wrong with you?" I handed him a glass of water, which he downed in a gulp.

After a bit, he drew a long breath and said, "I just got a call from my friend, my best friend. We've discussed you, and he knows a Korean-Chinese family. Several days ago, their daughter committed suicide, some kind of mental problem. But they are too poor to bury her and feel too shameful to talk about her death. My friend suggested they sell her ID to us instead of reporting her death to the local office; no one knows about it except her parents and brother. You could use her ID, have legal status, and be free. It'll be much easier to live here. And then, Jia, with that ID, you can go to another country, like South Korea. Do you know what I mean? You can get out of here. You can walk outside whenever you want. Everything will be fine. You don't ever have to be anxious again about being caught by the police."

I just watched his lips quietly for a while. "Is it easy to make her ID mine?"

He smiled, wiping the sweat that flew down from his forehead with the back of his hand. "I don't think it's so difficult. The mother said her hometown was also in North Korea and they still have relatives over there; they feel sorry for North Koreans. They already agreed to help you. You won't have any problems using her ID."

With a big smile, Hyunmi clapped her hands and said, "Oh, Jia! This is extremely good luck." Her eyes glittered.

I remained quiet, trying to take in the news. *I can go anywhere? I can have my own life?* My heart raced, and then raced some more.

17

A Sad Reunion

It took time for me to feel safe in my new identity. Having stayed with Jin for three months and learned a fair amount of Chinese, I had grown somewhat accustomed to life in China. Hyunmi told me her aunt was looking for an assistant chef for her restaurant, and suggested the job would be a good path to independence, as I could live with her aunt at the restaurant. I thought it was time for me to compensate Jin for his help, and this could be the first step. I was excited to settle into a new life.

I took a bus into the city and followed Hyunmi's directions to her aunt's restaurant. I noted the stores on the street as I passed them on foot; this area, I thought, might become my new neighborhood.

Suddenly, I felt a tap on my back. Afraid it might become a repeat of my disastrous search for Sangwon, I kept walking, but the person tapped my back again. I walked faster, but I could hear footsteps close on my heels. When I was about to run, a man's voice called my name in a low voice, "Jia! Jia!"

I looked back in surprise; who knew my name here? It was Gun. He looked much older than the last time I had seen him. I never expected that my wish to see him again would come true so soon. He seized my arm in haste and dragged me into a side street.

"Can I talk to you for a moment?"

"Gun, my God. Where have you been? I'm always thinking about you. You want to go to some place to talk?"

He looked around anxiously, pointed with his chin, and said, "Go down this street slowly and find the closest inn. Reserve a room. When you get the number of the room, say it loudly, as if you're making sure of it. I'll follow right behind you. I'll tap on the door three times in rapid succession, and then once more. Okay?"

As soon as he saw me nod my head, he disappeared. It was amazing to see him—I was so happy to run into him on the street. But why did he look so nervous? Why did he look so old?

I did as I was told. I walked straight down the street, slowly. I tried not to look back, pretending to look in storefront windows on the way. I tried to find him in the reflection from the windows, but he wasn't there.

I found the inn easily, and reserved a room. I repeated the room number three times loudly, as the inn owner looked at me curiously. I looked back on my way up to the third floor, but no one was following me. Locking the door to the room, I turned to find a small bed, a pink-flowered thermos on a nightstand, and a well-used washbasin. The smell of disinfectant assailed my nostrils. I perched on the bed's edge for over an hour, all my nervous energy focused on the door. I wondered how long I should wait. Had I really seen him? Was it Gun? Was I sleepwalking? I decided to wait a little longer. Another hour passed; it felt like a whole day. I was already late for my appointment with Hyunmi's aunt.

I stood up; I must have seen a phantom on the street, not Gun. The moment I walked toward the door to leave, there were three cautious knocks, then one more, exactly as he'd said. As soon as I opened the door, Gun swept in, locked the door, and plopped himself down on the floor.

"Are you okay? Gun—what's happened? Is someone chasing you? Gun? You can't imagine how happy I am to see you again."

He looked up at me and gave me a tight smile. "I wondered if it was really you when I saw you. When did you get here? You look good. You don't look like a North Korean woman at all. That's why I had to follow you for a while. It took time to figure it out."

He had always been dark, but his gloomy face made him seem even darker; his cheeks had sunk deep into the hollows below his cheekbones.

"I've been here several months," I told him excitedly. "How have you been? Do you live here? Oh—so many things to ask... How are your parents? Is everything all right?" As I spoke, his eyes darted back and forth.

He smiled bitterly and said, "My father is dead and my mother has been seriously sick since he passed away."

Putting down my bag, I sat next to him and grabbed his hand. "I'm so sorry, Gun. But I'm so happy to see you again in this life. Did you come back to China right after you visited your uncle's house?"

I wanted to ask about Sun—whether he had found her or not—but hesitated. I decided to bring up other topics that came to mind instead.

He slipped his hand out of mine. "Many things happened after that," he said darkly. He paused and kept his eyes on the ground. It became clear nothing had gone as he had planned. Who dared to make plans anymore? He raised his eyes to mine briefly and said, "I found Sun here too."

My body tensed when I heard Sun's name. I grabbed his hand again and squeezed it more tightly. "Where is she? Are you with Sun now? Can I see her?"

Gun just gave me a vacant stare. "You can't see her anymore."

Sun's Story II

As I clung to Gun's words, I realized that the fate I so hoped Sun would escape had in fact befallen her.

The night Sun left Pyongyang, she headed for Kaesant'un, a village close to the border. She'd been told that Kaesant'un was the place to cross the border by a Korean-Chinese vendor in a street market, a woman she had paid to help her. The journey had gone well; the last barrier was the river.

Sun saw some soldiers at the border chatting and smoking. She didn't know what to do, and waited for a while, hoping they would leave. The river didn't look as difficult to cross as she feared, but she knew stepping onto Chinese land was strictly prohibited. Sun had never violated the law in her life, and her legs were trembling. In that moment, Sun regretted not having told me where she was headed. I treated her as a younger sister, and she had been afraid I would not let her leave, or would tell her parents. If Sun had convinced me, though, I might have left with her; two would have been better than one. But it was too late for regrets.

She decided to wait until all the soldiers were gone. When they returned to their post to eat, she would have a chance to sneak into the river and swim across. The current looked a bit fast and the water was high, but the river wasn't too wide, and Sun was confident of her swimming skills. After crossing, she would look for Gun. The Korean-Chinese vendor had told her many North Koreans lived in Korean-Chinese villages and received help from Korean-Chinese people. She would go to Yanji, a city in China near the border, and ask for help.

While Sun waited for the appropriate time, she hid behind some buildings. She wondered how her parents were, and thought how disappointed they would be at her disappearance. She missed them so much. She waited, watching the sky. Cotton clouds floated smoothly overhead and into the distance over China. Sun sighed, thinking how good it would be to cross the river on those clouds.

Her mind drifted along for a time, and soon she was standing in the middle of an unfamiliar street. As she looked around to figure out where she was, she saw Gun walk past along a narrow curb. The road quickly filled with people walking quickly in the same direction. She tried to follow Gun, but she was shoved back and forth by the flood of human bodies and couldn't catch him. She called after him repeatedly. Suddenly, he turned back and their eyes met. She beckoned him to come toward her, but he only stared at her, as if at a stranger, before disappearing in the crowd. His figure grew smaller and smaller. She cried out again and again, but he was gone.

People passing by stopped and glared at Sun with red, unblinking eyes as big as half their faces.

With a startle, Sun awoke and came to her senses. She realized that she had called out to Gun in reality, not just in the dream. She felt chilled, and thought it might be night; she couldn't feel the sun or see the sky. Then, gaining her bearings, she realized that the daylight was being blocked by shadows looming over her. Dark faces moved down to hers—someone had heard her cry out in her dream.

The strange men wore uniforms and said they were soldiers, but they didn't arrest Sun. She was taken to a building near the border. They were polite to her, asking her why she wanted to go to China and whether she traveled alone or with others. She was too afraid to answer, but they gave her food and hot water and even asked her whether she needed money. She finally confessed that she was going to China to look for her boyfriend. They warned her how dangerous the place was for a woman, and told her it would be impossible to find her boyfriend by herself. They said they might help her and introduce her to some people over there. She was ecstatic—China would not be as scary as people said! After conversing with her for a while, one of the men left in a hurry.

Several hours later, the man returned with two others. One of them addressed her politely in Korean and told her that they could help her because they lived in China and took care of many North Koreans out of pity. She cried and thanked him profusely. They asked her how old she was, where she lived, and what job she had. They were angry when they heard about Gun abandoning her and criticized him harshly. She wasn't happy about that, but she appreciated their help nevertheless. Sun felt no one could be as lucky as she was.

She crossed the border with them safely—and she didn't have to swim, because they brought a small boat. They took her to a house where she could stay while they tried to find Gun. They gave her new clothes and cosmetics to prepare her for Gun's visit. Sun's heart overflowed with gratitude, and she gave all her money to them as a token of her appreciation. She was in a flutter, waiting for him.

Several days later, a man came to take her away from there, but the man who came was not Gun. He was a big, middle-aged Chinese man. Young, pretty, and unmarried, Sun was sold for 10,000 yuan. Her kidnappers were happy with the price. She didn't understand what was going on until the Chinese man dragged her to his car with a leer. Struggling to get away from him, she looked at her kidnappers in disbelief. They only snickered; one patted her on the hip and said, "He'll make you much happier than your stupid boyfriend." She writhed and yelled at them to release her from the fat Chinese man's grasp. But it was too late.

Gun's Story II

Gun took a cigarette from the pocket of his shirt. Recounting Sun's story to me had taken its toll on him; he looked tired and dejected. He lit the cigarette and took a few drags. When I had last seen him, he didn't smoke; now he had turned into a chain-smoker.

"If I hadn't been arrested… If I hadn't slept in my uncle's house that night… If I hadn't been stuck in that hell for three months, Sun might not have been subjected to that kind of life."

"What do you mean?" I asked. I didn't understand. "Where were you for three months? What happened to you in your uncle's house?" I tugged at his arm. What I had most feared would happen to Sun had already happened. "Where did you find Sun? Where is she now?"

I thought about the women who married Chinese men in that small village and were dragged back to North Korea. Is that what happened to Sun? Was that why Gun said I couldn't see her anymore?

Gun's eyes, misty with tears, gazed through me. He didn't answer my questions, but continued, "I found Sun at last. Since returning to China, my job has been to find people like us. Whenever I hear about North Koreans, I run to catch them. I was driven by the desperate hope to see Sun's face again, and I searched bars, karaoke places, restaurants—everywhere. I hoped I wouldn't find her in those kinds of places, but as time passed, I realized that finding her at all would be a miracle.

"When I finally saw her, seven months after arriving in China, I wanted to tear my heart to shreds. I heard one village in Heilongjiang had several North Korean women living with Chinese men. I had visited many villages, pursuing similar rumors, with no luck. But I went to the village and checked on all of the women. I couldn't find her. As I was about to leave, I stopped by a small, dirty grocery store, and asked the old woman there if she knew of Sun. She told me about a pathetic girl from North Korea who was locked in a madman's house, and gave me directions. I headed there, thinking, *It can't be Sun. She can't be so unlucky.* When I got to the house, I threatened the man that I would turn him in to the police if he didn't show me his wife."

Gun's eyes seemed to dive into the sea. Then he scowled fiercely, looking away.

"The door to her room was locked. When I was let inside, she didn't recognize me. She tried to run away—she thought I was going to hurt her. She just squatted in the corner, and wailed when I tried to touch her. She was like an animal. She had bruises all over her body. When I spoke her name, she stopped crying and raised her head slightly, watching my face with fear. As soon as she registered my face, she shrank back to her place in the corner, crying without a sound. I just repeated, "Sun, I'm back. I'm back. You don't have to worry anymore." She didn't stop crying and wouldn't look at me.

"At that moment, the Chinese man came into the room and told me to get out. Sun tried to interfere, but he pushed her to the floor. I was furious. I ran to her and tried to stand her up, but she pushed me back as soon as I touched her. Everything was a blur. He shouted at me to leave. I seized his arm and we left the room together. Turning back to Sun, I told her I wasn't leaving, to wait there for a moment. From outside the room I could hear her wailing."

As I listened to him, my body began shaking.

Gun continued without looking at me. "I told the Chinese man that Sun was my sister, that I had been sent to get her back from him. He sneered at me, realizing that I wouldn't turn him in to the Chinese police. He said that for 15,000 yuan he would let her go. I promised to get him the money and warned him not to touch her before I returned, or he'd get nothing.

"I hesitated to say goodbye to Sun; it seemed she might die of desolation. I told her I'd be back soon, and she stopped sobbing and became quiet. Jia, you don't know how much I cried on the way back from the house; people on the street thought I was crazy. I was angry at my country, my cousin, and that place. But more than anyone, I was angry with myself." He raised his head and looked at the ceiling for a moment. Gray molding decorated each corner of the ceiling.

"It took a week to gather the money. When I returned

and put the money in the man's hand, he said, 'I told her she'd soon be free, but she doesn't want to leave. Anyway, it's your responsibility to take her out of my house. If she refuses to leave, it's not my fault. Don't expect me to give the money back if she doesn't go with you. I gave you a chance.'

"I entered the room where Sun was kept. She looked much calmer. She began to relate what she had experienced and how she had been defiled by the Chinese bastard. I tried to stop her; I didn't want her to relive the pain, and I didn't want to hear it either. I begged her to leave with me, but she was so stubborn. She said she wouldn't move one step from that place. I cried in disbelief. She cried too, but she wouldn't change her mind.

"I understood why she refused to leave. Her eyes were filled with fear and shame. I talked and talked to her, trying to convince her that nothing was her fault—that she should blame the world, not herself. She listened silently, and I didn't try to force her. I said I would be back in several days. I wanted to give her some time to think. I was so sure she would change her mind and leave with me. That was my biggest, most terrible mistake."

Gun paused. He watched me with sad eyes, then suddenly bent his head down and rubbed the floor with his fingers. It was filthy, but he didn't care.

"When I returned to the house, she was dead. The Chinese man blankly told me she'd killed herself. I went out of my mind. I refused to believe it; I was sure he was trying to get more money from me. I grabbed his shirt and threatened him, but he shouted and his neighbors came. They confirmed that they had seen Sun's dead body. I asked the man where her body was, and he said he had buried it somewhere in the hills because he thought I wouldn't come back, and because her body had turned black from the poison that she took. He ranted about her. He complained that he'd wasted too much money on her and that I should pay for the medicine she had taken every day to control her headaches and her insanity. Without it, he said, she would have cried out and hit her head against the wall all day.

"I was speechless. I looked at him for a long time. He wasn't human. He warned me not even to think of getting my money back and threw a bag at me, saying it was the only thing she'd left behind. Then he disappeared hastily with his friends. I opened the bag and found Sun's belongings well organized inside. She had packed her things neatly in preparation for getting out of that hell. It did not make sense that she would kill herself while waiting for me to come for her.

"As I stood in front of the house in a trance, a Korean-Chinese woman living next door cautiously approached me. She said there had been a big fight the night I left, and she had heard Sun cry out as he beat and harassed her. The woman expressed her regret and said she hadn't dared to stop him.

"I was so stupid. If I hadn't given him money, she'd still be alive. I thanked the woman for telling me the truth. Later that night, I returned to the Chinese man's house. I beat the bastard to death and burned his house down."

Gun had finished his pack of cigarettes. We looked at each other in silence, and my eyes filled with tears. I remembered my last night with Sun in Pyongyang; if only I had tried to persuade her not to cross the border to find Gun. If I had at least shown that I knew of her plan to leave, she might have lived.

Gun's eyes were full of guilt and self-loathing. He

seemed to be waiting for me to punish him. But how could I say everything was his fault? How could I blame him for killing an innocent and lovable girl? If he was the one who had let her die, I was an accomplice.

Gun broke the silence between us, rubbing his dirty fingers on his pants. "One thing I envy you is that you still remember Sun when she was pretty, and talked tirelessly all day, with her bright smile. I can't remember that face anymore. The vision of her imprinted on my brain is a bruised face, with sunken eyes and a broken nose."

Suddenly, he chuckled and shrugged his shoulders. "But, Jia, you know what? You know what I'm doing here right now?" He looked directly into my eyes. "I'm a spy. I'm an agent who hands people like us over to the government. As soon as I get some information about North Koreans here, I give it to the North Korean police. Then they arrest them and send them back to North Korea. I'm catching people who run away, just as I did."

He crumpled his empty cigarette box.

"Jia, do you know how I got enough money to give to that Chinese bastard? I threatened North Korean women living here, sometimes families. I told them I would turn them over to North Korean agents if they wouldn't give me money. I forced the money out of them. A few of them I beat. I used them to save Sun."

I was incredulous. I glared at him with my eyes wide.

"You asked where I was for three months? I was in prison. I was tortured and trained to be a secret agent, to catch North Koreans in China." His gloomy eyes looked into mine. "Don't worry—I'm not going to turn you in. They found my father and mother in China while I was in prison. They told me they would protect them if I cooperated; otherwise, I wouldn't see my parents again in this life. My father died, but they still have my mother. I don't know where she is right now from the letters they hand me regularly; I only know she's not dead yet."

Feeling concern for him, I asked, "Are you okay here, with me? Isn't it dangerous?"

Gun looked at the door for a moment. "They already suspect me and keep a close watch on me—that's why I was so cautious in meeting with you. I've stopped giving them information about North Koreans. When they realize I'm not useful to them anymore, they'll take me back to prison. Who knows when? Maybe tomorrow!" He laughed absentmindedly.

I walked out of the room. My brain needed some fresh air. I told Gun I would bring back something for us to drink.

The street was filled with people, as usual. There were many women Sun's age, walking quickly, dressed in their finest. Some girls laughed loudly with their friends, others walked arm in arm with their boyfriends, broad smiles on their faces. A distance of a few miles meant a world of difference between their fates and the fates of Sun and Gun.

Sun had always spoken brightly of her future, what she would do, how she would live. How different were the circumstances of her death. Is this world fair at all? I was sure, when Sun finally met up with Gun in China, that she must have been heartbroken and confused. What happened to her was not her fault; she must have been wracked with shame. It was shame that prevented her from leaving right away, though her instinct was to escape with Gun as soon as possible. I understood her desperation, the struggle taking place in her mind. I imagined her resolving to start life anew with Gun, how happy she must have been packing her things that night. I couldn't stop crying.

I had often dreamed of their happy reunion somewhere in China. I even imagined running into them on the street, or in a store; completely free of starvation, unafraid of being caught for our "crimes." We would meet in an ice-cream parlor and talk about our futures, enjoying the sweet flavors.

It could only be a dream. Walking back to the inn with two bottles of water, I thought about how much Gun had changed and how he had tortured himself. I didn't know what to do with him. Should I urge him to think of his own safety from now on? Could I tell him about my own luck? My sadness and despair at losing Sun would only make him feel more guilty and desperate. I knew I couldn't lose Gun as well. I needed to pull him out of the hell he had descended into. Kind words from a friend would help him. I hastened back to the inn.

Opening the door with the brightest face I could muster, I found the room empty. Gun was already gone. He left only a note:

> Jia,
>
> I caused everything. I realize that it's not our fortune to guide our own lives. I was the one who killed her. I don't exist anymore. I don't breathe anymore. I'm not a living being anymore.
>
> Gun

I hurried outside and ran wildly down the street searching for him. I wanted to tell him that it wasn't his fault; he needed to hear those words just as Sun had. We were not just victims, but also survivors. I wanted to remind him that we are living, here and now. This is what we must hold on to.

But he had vanished as quickly as he came. I remained frozen there, on the busy street, for what seemed like hours, searching the faces of passersby.

About the Author

Hyejin Kim has written for numerous publications, including Asia Times. She has a Ph.D. in global affairs from Rutgers University. In 2003 she received the Korean Novelist Association's award for Best Television Drama Scenario. Jia was inspired by her human rights work with North Korean refugees in northern China.